PUPPIES

Puppies

JOHN VALENTINE

First published in the US in 1979
This edition published 1988 by GMP Publishers Ltd

World Copyright ©1988 John Valentine

Distributed in North America by
Alyson Publications Inc.,
40 Plympton Street, Boston, MA 02118, USA
telephone: (617) 542 5679

British Library Cataloguing in Publication Data

Valentine, John
   Puppies.
   I. Title
   813'.54(F)

   ISBN 0-85449-094-9

Cover Illustration by Phil Daniels
Printed and bound in the EC by Nørhaven A/S, Viborg, Denmark

EDITOR'S NOTE

Puppies is a collection of journal entries. It is not a story, and will disappoint anyone who seeks beginning, middle, and end. The book is full of ends, beginnings, and middles, but as in real life they do not occur in any particular order. Read the book instead as you would read a private diary: in quick, prying bursts, glancing over your shoulder occasionally for fear of being caught in the act.

CONTENTS

ONE

1969 – 1965

11/23/69 — Los Angeles

Moon waxing full. Cold for the time. The bullet that sang
diagonally across my room tonight was meant, I'm sure, to
do no more than that. If it had been intended to sting me on
that diagonal, it would have done. Bullets are generally quite
successful in their way—as I am not in mine—and this bullet,
especially, gave the impression of having been exactly placed.
Smug. Offensively confident.

All it had to do & did was cross the room & make me
thoughtful. Didn't even scare me: a snap outdoors, crack
(window), rip of air (first bells of falling glass) and thud into
the wall before the first shards hit the floor—too quick to
fear. (Earthquakes don't bother me, either: gone before I
know enough to fear. It's slow things terrify me—cancer,
time: the faggots of Hollywood Boulevard—their laughter
(not to hear them laugh) their eyes.)

Living in the Book of Revelation and waiting (waiting,
and) always no thing happening, you learn a bent rhetoric of
fear, gone bored of Apocalypse.

But I don't know anybody here/now who might think I
could use a slanting bullet. I'm quite anonymous in this Hollywood a half-block off the light. With the Panthers I'm cool,
the revolution has lost my number, there's nothing scheduled
this side of New Year's Day—no violence. Then who?

I don't think it could have been silver, that bullet. I don't
think I care.

Waxing full, the moon, and astronauts returning to sea this dawning day. A conjuration maybe. Maybe sex with any stranger. Or I'm full of speed & horny without flesh: horny to see or touch or, and incompetent. Wherefore I write or walk and think at the trodden moon or anyone against some wall leaning at precisely such an angle of display. Abstract lusts are easiest to burn.

I live almost wholly within my own head, but when I was two or three times younger than I am, I always knew the reason I did things, anything, and whenever somebody asked "What are you doing that for?" or "Why are you doing that?!" or even "What are you doing?" always I was able to explain it all so perfectly, I usually managed to consummate the act while still explaining it. All my friends & I learned more in this way than we'd ever meant to, and said less about it all than usual: high school wisdom of our sort, and proud of it.

Time spent answering most questions is freetime for your speechless parts, time out under mental business, and I grew up an explainer. Odd thing. I have heard myself explaining things I didn't understand and being right. Appalling & ulterior trait.

Now, of course, I don't know anymore why I do most any given thing, except sometimes when it's wholly a technical matter, and that infrequently. Why, for a guess, do I sometimes play the middle F-sharp of my recorder with left index & middle fingers, and other times with thumb alone? I say it has to do with phrasing, but I lie.

I forget—I have forgotten—why I do things; forget as well why I've forgotten. Naturally, I can explain that so much has passed in long practice from adroit to reflexive, has become so familiar it needn't be thought of, so near automatic that thought would impair it—which is a fine explanation, for being so nearly pure bullshit.

Sex, now: why do I practice the weird kind of sex I usually do, instead of the weird kind of sex I prefer? Or why, having soundly disliked children since I was one, have I come to manhood with the instincts of a child molester? What c'd be more sexless & icky than a 12-year-old, or more absurd than balling one? And what temptation could be harder to resist—or, blessed be, more rare? Eleven years ago I learned to live clear of situations likely to provide opportunities for such nonsense: no more motel managing, no more teaching school, no summer camps, no long propinquities.

Because, except to ball, I can't stand 12-year-olds, and 12-year-olds invariably talk, and they're singularly unrewarding lays.

And yet . . .

It may be I've forgotten how come I'm so perverse the better to enjoy perversity. Or maybe just to spare myself knowing just how horribly perverse I really am. My inner heart fears I may be disgusting, but as long as I don't know this, no one else is likely to find out.

But I'm not driven to little kids, and, away from dangerous situations, find temptation no job to avoid. Twelve-year-olds on playgrounds or streetcorners do not turn me on. (A New York friend of mine, John Camden, is not so fortunate, and Manhattan is a prepubescent hothouse. John has paid jail time for his fancies.)

Kids just a little older, on the other hand, from first down through the tag end of youth, kids 14 or so & up, say— whom also it is most uncool to fuck—kids tear me nerve from limb when I'm around them or in sight of them, wherefore even more so I avoid the situations above mentioned and their like.

I'm, much against my will, a heavily moral man, meaning

in this case I try not to take exceptional advantage or be in a position to, even unconsciously, apply unfair pressure, right? Even so, I've been known to force my attentions upon fairly helpless kids—but be it said that other kids have forced their attentions on me.

But I've arranged my life so that the kids I'm exposed to —and they to me—are all pretty much on their own & hip to what's happening. This—especially in the cities I've inhabited & here—isn't difficult. If I must be a dirty old man—and apparently I must—at least I can be the kind of d.o.m. I can like.

(But ask me how come this thing for kids & listen to me gliblip an explanation to you, though I've no idea anymore myself.)

Now, however, to complicate my cluttered life, the paper's bookkeeper, Jane, is pressing upon me her 16-year-old son Steven, who wants to learn newspaper production & magick &c from me, and who is aesthetically admirable. This in the waxing full of the moon. And how, in such a case, I shall maintain morality, or decorum, or discretion, is more puzzling than a bullet cutting through the office air aslant from God knows where/whom.

Prolonged close & intimate association with each other sh'd be instructive to us both, but pray God not to Jane.

4/8/71 — L.A.

Life without feeling is the American dream. Passionless fucking on nudebar stages and passionless killing in Benedict Canyon are flowers from the same bush. Police budget increases and welfare cuts are words & music of a single song. To live without feeling: even—and people desire it. Anesthesia. Christopher's problem is the American Way.

Alienation: is that what it's called?

I w'd expect that people w'd do ever more & more bizarre things in hopes of shocking some feeling into themselves. And that's what they're doing, but not for that reason.

> There was an old person from Yost
> Who had an affair with a ghost.
> At the height of the spasm
> The poor ectoplasm
> Shrieked, "Goodie! I feel it—almost!"

I was balling a lad who, when he came, was genuinely distressed because he almost never came, hadn't expected to come, didn't think he liked coming, and anyhow preferred not to.

I thought in getting his cock sucked he was taking an awful chance on coming, but what I said was, "Don't you *ever* come?"

"Only when I jerk off."

I didn't pursue the matter.

That was six years ago, and I didn't recognize The News Before It Happens when I heard it.

I was never able to induce Xtopher to come, except once (sort of) by hand, and I wonder if, as a rule, he ever does. 31 complains he's unwilling to come anywhere but in the cunt, and I wonder if she has any evidence besides behavior that he even comes there.

(I, on the other hand, c'd barely restrain myself. He had only to touch me and I was ready to pop, and the twice he blew me he nearly drowned.)

I've had an amazing number of uncoming puppies the past two years, compared to only one in all the years before. Even TW, for all the many times we've worked on it, for all his eagerness, is highly come-resistant.

But male orgasm is physiologically so easily induced that, till recently, it didn't even require the orgasmee's cooperation. Given intent & erection, orgasm's technically inevitable. Not any more.

Are we having an epidemic of male frigidity? (Does inability to come reflect an inability to give of oneself, to let oneself go?) What is this numb drought all about?

If 2 out of 5 of my puppies come, I think myself lucky. But the other three—why are they even willing to ball at all?

31 has noticed the same thing, both of Xtopher and in general, and adds that it's almost exclusively a youth problem. That is, in men 30+ it's unknown, in those 25- it's fairly common. She tried as usual to drum up an astrological explanation (which—my complaint against astrology—w'd prevent

our seeing the phenomenon in any useful context, as a part of a whole, from which information might be developed, conclusions drawn, and some idea had of the flow of change and possible shape of the future: the standard astrological dead end), then went on to blame speed, and then masturbation.

I threw a change on the matter and got:

45		51	
— —		= =	45. Gathering Together
———	9	= =	51. Arousing
= =	6	———	

telling me how to overcome the condition in my own puppies (by taking pains to arouse them to the moaning point before engaging) but not, I think, what it's all about.

Now, exactly one year later, I see that oracle differently. It sounds like an approaching cataclysm for which the Tao is preparing the species to survive. I don't know what male frigidity c'd be preparing us for, except maybe a population crisis. But, from the evidence around me, it w'd seem that girl babies are markedly outnumbering boy babies, which suggests just the opposite.

Either way, we're being groomed for the fall of Atlantis.

2/22/70 — L.A.

Fuckingwise, 2222 Endor Park was passing dull. There was, briefly, Balzac. Chris Molatin. James Bennett, from whom I got Bardon's *Initiation into Hermetics*, but unsatisfactory sex. Then in August Brian Slint, now a New York cop, who didn't like being fucked but allowed it, why I know not. Robin Metsky, the 15-year-old from Pennsylvania whose cherry I dedicated to Ashtoreth.

During the same period, at Libbi and Jim's, there was Gary Thong, a gregarious Gemini metalworker whom Amy'd also enjoyed, who was living with Judy Milan, whom I balled shamelessly but inconclusively 9/11 only, whom nobody's seen since. (Great pity, that. A fine, masculine bisexual, smart & lovable, perfect candidate for 'roommate', gone without a trace. Shit. We agreed to meet at Morloch's the next evening, and it never happened.) Also Poohbear, one of Bishop's Coven, Aquarius, a truly luxury puppy, lush, a puppy for all senses— purely recreational, but superior recreation.

Gary, Poohbear & Robin were all picked up at the Magical Mystery Museum. Occult fringe benefits.

Moved in Sept/Oct to Rivendell, one of many, near Hywd & Western. Zero sex. Had—as I'd had since mid-August—Allen Greenwood as inseparable roommate & adamant non-ball.

Then in October moved to *Tuesday's Child* office on Argyle near Hywd & Vine. A decaying 1-story cardboard office building mostly occupied by a *Free Press* street distribution center & related streetpeople enterprises. Peeling wallpaper. Broken windows. Unlockable locks. Bad plumbing. Most slumlike quarters I've ever had.

Worked and slept in rear office. Furniture: desk & chair; electric heater; desk lamp; two unwholesome thin plastic-covered pads 6 feet long by 1½ wide for a bed, along with a couple of grimy blankets, a pillow or two, and 50 bundles of *Tuesday's Child*, 100 to the bundle. Forget about bathing. And in the office adjoining, also rented by *TC*, behind an inside door without lock or knob, Allen Greenwood lived. Really deplorable conditions. (In the absence of any kind of curtaining, I had newspapers taped over the windows.)

It was a sexual paradise.

Because of the location, mainly. Hywd Blvd one block uphill, Sunset one block down, a block east of Vine, three blocks from the Hywd Ranch Market, on the corner of Selma. Densest per-block stray pup population in America. Most intense meatrack this side of Times Square, but relaxed. A million pups looking for someplace to crash. A million others hustling. Another million looking to get laid. And a third as many chicks, most going steady.

And the *Free Press* operation in the front of the building was main source of income for a majority of the street kids. They supported themselves selling the Freep on the street, and this building was their supplier. That's why *TC* rented space there to begin with—to be close to the street dealers. We knew we weren't going to make it on subscriptions.

The building was the streetkids' social & community center. Anyone looking for a crashpad looked first there.

I caught one puppy in the donut shop on Vine near the Ranch Market. Another kid I saw across the street as I left the coffeehouse one morning. He went up Highland to Fountain

& east, and I followed him, for he was one pretty puppy. When I finally caught up with him & said Good Morning or some such shit, he asked where the YMCA was. I told him & asked why. Because you can sometimes get a dormitory bed there for $2. I colorfully deprecated YMCA dorms. He agreed. I said if he needed a place to crash, he c'd use my office, since I was going to have to work all night. He said You're not a queer or something, are you? and explained how scared he was of queers. I solemnly assured him I was not a queer.

At the office I laid out the pads for him. Advantage of the pads: so narrow that if they're laid parallel, as they had to be in that space, and there's a body on each pad, the bodies must touch each other.

Turned off the overhead, turned on my desk lamp. Pup unshod & crashed. I wrote magick article for *TC*.

Pup was 19 or so. Shorter than I, six inches at least. Sturdy & well-developed. Darkish, possibly part Indian. From Montana. Cowboyish. Cashiered out of Marines for dope. Working as after-hours janitor in a bar on LaBrea.

When he was asleep, I turned off my light, undressed, and oozed onto the narrow pad beside him. An arm laid gently across him, so gradually introduced it had always been there. Light stroking—at once both for pleasure & for exploration. He's good to stroke. Soft/firm, smooth, warm, stirring a little under my hand. All casual as dreams.

A foray crotchward finds an alert erection and the masquerade is over.

I undress him very slowly, like unwrapping a present, enjoying every particle of the process. The muffled snap of buttons loosed, the sliding of the shirt up that smooth way &, savoring, over the head & off of the quasi-dormant arms (passive, but lighter than deadweight). A *good*—i.e., pleasant—

not quite clean smell—as of a shower yesterday morning. The
usual complications at the belt buckle, vain struggle to open
it, a hassle—then his hands charmingly sneaking in to solve the
buckle with one practiced motion & then sneaking off again
to play dormant, though he's blown his cover & there's no
deception possible now.

Freeing the hips from the tubular Levis. He humps his ass
dormantly to ease them down. It's like a pile of dirty clothes
giving birth to a puppy. Down the columns of his legs—smooth
to touch & the hair soft. Taking care the pants don't bunch
up & get awkward to remove. Past the knees, nearing ankles.
He hadn't counted on nakedness, but you can feel his mind
change in the texture of his calves. Then over the ankles & up
off the feet & tossed cavalierly behind me to the floor. Peel
off the stockings as well.

Unexpectedly naked youth with hardon, a la carte.

Flow back up the tree of his body, taking it by inches &
claiming it. To the swell of thighs & in to cock. Handle same,
deal lovingly therewith, promising, and flow on, hands devour-
ing contours, the delicate geometry of boy in his fullness:
muscles, sheathed ribs, token hair, different-grained bumps of
nipple, the abundant deltoids, the coarser thatch of armpit,
the sphere of shoulder, throat & nape, that jaw, those ears,
this forehead, hair. He hadn't expected to be kissed, either.
Certainly he hadn't expected to kiss back.

Plastered skin to skin, tongue to tongue, we fuck slowly.
The heater lights the room low red. His cock is pressed tight
against my belly, and is pulsing. My hands search out his
nerves, learn their pattern, scheme a program.

God, this feels good!

Down now in slow sweeps to crouch over his panicky
cock. Rub inside thighs—softly, with fingertips & slightly

nails. Stroke the legs like stroking animals. Slide charged fingers across his belly, solar plexus, chest. Suck a nipple. Get a hand down between his legs, finger his buttocks like cantaloupes, insert a brief fingertip in rectum & massage the thick cord at his Muladhara chakra, toy with his balls, grasp the rod & sink down on it, tongue swarming, saliva saved up for now bubbles back & forth across the head. We reach bedrock & stay there, grasping balls with one hand & a nipple with the other.

Oh! he says, surprised.

How come surprised? He must have known when I first groped him he was likely to get sucked.

This is a night, and this is a boy, for doing it slowly & in much detail. More than 45 minutes of blowing. Bringing him up to the brink & easing off, again & again, each a more perilous brink, a more unlikely retreat, he the while moaning & ah-ing quite noisily (I find I *like* a noisy fuck), I taking all manner of other advantage of him the while. I've given him a long fingerwave whilst he said No, don't, no, oh, oh. I've rubbed my paws repeatedly over every square inch of his glorious body (the Marines build men). I've rubbed my cock against his leg, a nether fuck, almost beyond recovery. And now he has said cock of mine in his hand & is doing enlightened things to it.

In sucking, I have used loose & tight, down & up through the whole range of speeds. I have employed tongue, teeth & spittle imaginatively. I have rotated & shaken. I have sucked at most of my possible vacuums, and have likewise blown at divers pressures. I have turned his cock every way but loose. And he is panting heavily, and my jaw is getting tired, and this time

I
WON'T
STOP IT   a Roman candle of come, lots of squishing &
sloshing, bass-drum beat of his frenzied ass against the floor
(through 1½ inches of padding), he vocalizing ecstasy. Enormous pressure of bursting cock against my soft palate, Bright
Sparks Behind My Eyes, aborted gag reflex, and the spurt
spurt of hot semen, a smell a bit like Clorox, coming faster
than I can swallow (tastes slightly tart), running out of my
mouth & down his cock to irrigate his boyhair. (I suppose
this is an acquired taste.) And I coming in his hand the while.

Then we lay there, breathing hard but otherwise not
moving. Yes. He said Wow, and I Ummm. I slid up beside
him on the pad again, put my arms all around him, and we
slept that way.

We didn't mention it later, but he didn't seem unhappy.
We've met in passing several times since with great friendliness.

I wonder what he'll do if he ever runs into a queer? (And
what precisely is he afraid of, if not what I gave him?)

Or Tex, a kid who showed up at the office one day asking
for work, food, a place to crash, whatever. Tall & skinny, a
look I like though it's not what I can call pretty. Demented—
either a pathological liar or delusive. Lies about vast sums of
money readily available to him for the asking, about his
famous &/or tough friends, about his own physical prowess
(karate bullshit)— and probably about everything else as well.

He's dirty, very. And broke. His clothes are falling apart.
Besides being demented, he's a mite stupid. For my usual
purposes, all this is immaterial.

Light hair, blue eyes, Texas way of talking. Clearly still a
boy.

Anyhow, not yet even scheming, I tell him he can flop in the office, and go back to my work. (Oh yes, he's also on reds, if he speaks sooth.) So he flops.

A while later I turn around & realize I have a puppy asleep on my floor. I sit on a stack of newspapers beside him & look him over. I note all his sanitary defects & disregard them. I theorize that he probably has crabs & disregard that also. This takes a long time, just staring at this sleeping boychild.

I don't know why, but instead of my usual protracted approach I reach over, unzip his fly, lay firm hold of his cock, and proceed to rub & roll & press & maul it systematically to erection. This is a strange procedure for me. Generally I like to consolidate each gain thoroughly, and enjoy it for a while, before going on to the next, ideally working with such finesse that the transition from sleep to sex is hardly perceptible to my guest. This time I just plunged in & barged ahead without regard for Tex's possible reactions.

There are exceptions, but in general a properly stimulated cock (with special attention to thumbpressing the head) will rise to attention regardless of its owner's will in the matter. (At that, most puppies seem to regard their cock's will as their own, and do as it bids.) In my line, it is axiomatic that a hardon signifies consent. If you get your hand to ground zero & find an erection, you're cool. Sometimes it will give a little jump when you discover it. (Eddie Bronson, the first time, did that—a very sharp jump—and I was delighted: knew what that meant right away.) A flaccid cock that can be roused is likewise implied consent, on the theory that whatever it took to rouse the cock very likely roused the boy as well, and if he hasn't stopped you, it's because he hasn't wanted you to stop. (The exceptions to this are very trying.)

In this case, such considerations were irrelevant. As soon

as it understood what was up, Tex's penis turned to stone. Tex continued to pretend sleep. That was his business.

With the atypical frontal approach, the engineering peculiarities of belt & pants offered no problems. Got his pants off quicker'n I c'd've got my own off. (As usual, he blew his sleep-cover by humping his ass to help me get his pants down. It is only common courtesy to repay such consideration by going along with the sleep pretense for as long as he chooses.)

I did then give mad young Tex a most proficient blowjob, and then, done, eased his pants back into place, left belt & fly a-gape, and returned to my work, as he to his slumber. As though he were a semen-dispensing machine & I had just taken time off for a cock break.

Next day I brought him out to the Riverside house (Lardbutt was still in residence) to, I planned, feed him & wash him (he was a bit rank) & do it again. Got him fed. Got him into the bathtub. Couldn't get him out again. Had foolishly given him 2 tabs of methedrine, and now he waxed both mad & talkative, and stayed the whole day soaking in the tub & rapping dementia.

A few weeks later, though, under much the same conditions as before, except that this time he was expecting it—it was what he was there for—we did it again.

One Sunday night on Hywd Blvd, at the corner of Argyle (I had just then stepped out to see if there were, against the odds, somebody to play with), I was picked up by a Marine. Good specimen. Well done. He asked me how to get to Camp Something by bus. I told him I didn't know, adding that since it was after 2 AM there were probably no busses running anyway. He expressed dismay & need of sleepplace. I volunteered as usual.

Walking back to the pad he gave me the impression that he'd dig getting blown, but never said as much. I took note but made no overt response. Seducing someone who's already willing is a playful challenge. I got him laid out & studied Qabalah until he was evidently asleep, then crept in the sack beside him.

The exploratory process was shorter than I like. That is, he let me get my jollies manually for a while, but when I got to crotch & made the expected discovery, his cooperation precluded further foreplay, and we got right down to business.

Mostpeople accept fellatio passively. They lie there motionless until the orgasm reflex overwhelms them. This is foolish: bad sex, bad art & a mindless drag. If you're willing to have your cock sucked, you sh'd be willing to participate. Fellatio, after all, is just another form of fucking; the suckee sh'd by right & reason *fuck*. Lying rigid while a busy mouth passes up & down your cock is masturbation; moving with it, treating that mouth like a variant cunt & properly fucking it, is mature sex. The movement is part of the act—sex isn't just genitalia. Movement enhances & intensifies the pleasure. Even in old-fashioned manual masturbation, if instead of rubbing your cock like a dead stick, moving naught but your hand, if instead you keep your hand relatively still & move your cock with the pelvic thrusts of normal intercourse, if instead of rubbing your cock you fuck your hand, the result is immeasurably superior to what you'd expect, playing solitaire. But since mostpeople get sucked passively, hardly anyone realizes that fellatio can be very good sex. However, we fellators have come to accept what we can get & make do. It's hard to teach people in the act, and few will listen before (or after).

This Marine was not the passive type. He didn't get sucked,

he fucked me in the mouth. A fine, solid, grown-up lay, satis-factory in all respects to all concerned. Intelligent fucking. His purpose was pleasure, and he worked toward that end & got it.

But he wouldn't do it again, damn it. Rolled over & went to sleep. Split in the morning, saying Thanx & Later, never to be found again.

There was a little blond friend of Laszlo Scott's whom I ripped off from a coffeeshop at Vine & Sunset one cold morning, aged 16, and brought home to read my *High Tea* essay on Laszlo. He crashed & I violated him as usual. Passive, but my activity somewhat compensated. Like oddly many of my Argyle boys, he had good-tasting semen. Fringe benefit.

Two kids, 15 & 16, I found in great need (freezing cold windy night) on the steps of the building. The younger made a point of mentioning *Myra Breckenridge* (Gore Vidal novel), was surprised I'd not read it, so went on to clarify that he liked to read about homosexuals. I considered that suggestive enough for a family magazine, but the other kid, a runaway from the midwest, had altogether different vibes, and I pon-dered how to fuck the one without freaking the other.

They crashed. I crashed a long while after. Old pads crowded with three bodies.

Both kids were street urchins. Both sorely needed baths, change of clothing, &c. Both very pretty.

If I lay mostly on the floor & used the pad for a pillow, there was just room for me to ease in close to the suggestor. Did so.

This put most of the puppy above my head. So I started in a fairly common sleeping attitude with my head cradled in my arms, from which my hands evolved upward to paydirt. Paydirt gave his tacit consent to increasingly less tentative inroads on his person. Hands inside his clothes roaming freely through his glades & groves. But he remained lying on his side, facing away from me.

My hands entered his trousers & were welcome there. They took unimpeded liberties with his private parts. They remarked upon his neat hard cock & easy balls. They overcame the standard packaging difficulties & exposed his trove to view—but still he lay on his side, even resisted my efforts to roll him over.

I catch on slowly.

When I did, I stripped down, moistened my tool, and slid it up his teenage arse neat as sword in scabbard. Friend Paydirt either had a remarkably large & open anus, or remarkable sphincter control or an awful lot of experience for a 15-year-old. I still haven't learned how to be rogered comfortably, and I dig being rogered. And most of the arses I've plumbed have had difficulties similar to my own. But Paydirt's rectum opened like a supermarket door & sucked me in. And not at all loose. And with naught but spit to lubricate.

It was a good place to be. I liked it there. I fucked as well as I knew how, appreciatively. Honored him by taking him fully, as one would a woman. Deep, long strokes, rotations. Full fuck. Yay full fuck! Whilst one hand ranged his sleek body playing neural games, the other dwelt upon his new-grown cock, giving it as nearly as could be the equivalent of what I was getting. Managing despite some inexperience to produce simultaneous orgasms, a grace note.

Not as prolonged as I'd've liked. Unaccustomed as I am to such fine arseholes, I came not too soon but sooner than I wanted.

And all of this in total silence, lest we wake his partner.

Paydirt split at daybreak, solo, never to return. Now I was tempted to have a go at his abandoned partner, but I resisted. Later I regretted that.

There was Chuck Carney, Aries, 19, from S. Dakota. I encountered him in the hall by the john. (The john was at my end of the building. By keeping my door open, I c'd monitor all john traffic from my desk.) I froze, stunned, first time I saw him. Pale, pale blue eyes, pale silver-blond hair, faded Levi jeans & jacket, tall, virile, with an idealized body & a SmilE. He went into the john while I stood in my door, shocked. A good, long, copious, noisy piss.

He left the john, walked like a panther to the front of the building, and back, and forth again. Next trip back—he was obviously pacing—I asked if I c'd help him. I sure could. He was waitin' to meet someone & they was late & c'd he stash his jacket in my office while he went out & got him somethin' to eat? Yes he could.

While he was gone I performed a magical operation on his jacket designed to bring him back & into my bed. Elixir Vitae was one of the ingredients.

Came back, we talked. He threw a few changes (subject: The Draft). People he was waiting for never showed. He ended up crashing in my pad by default. If the people'd shown up, he'd've gone off with them to some chick's crashpad/commune in the wilds of the Wilshire district.

I c'd barely believe there was such a beautiful boy animal sleeping on my two dirty mattresses, helpless prey to whatever of my carnal whims he might choose to tolerate. An awesome body. His paleness & sheen glowed. He was a moon in my dim office. I sat for hours looking/staring at him before I moved.

Went to bed & started to develop the assets. He was at first somewhat resistant—turning out from under a hopefully placed hand, once lightly brushing a hand away. As though in his sleep, unconsciously. I took the greater possibility that he was no longer really sleeping, merely pretending, to be encouraging. (In choosing to feign sleep he has entered into the game. Onward.) Resistant at first, and then reluctant, but not reluctant enough to tell me to lay off.

(I think these inadequate reluctances to be, usually, self-justification rites. Theory being that if you resisted but he overcame your resistance, that proves you're in no way responsible for the events that follow, leaving you free to enjoy yourself without guilt. Like the typist & her glass of beer: "He got me drunk & took advantage of me." Or David Jornad & the Dexedrine heart. Or most puppies & dope.

(I can't prove this, but I submit: every time I have ever been offered genuine resistance, I have withdrawn. Whenever I have been told "Stop that"—alas—I have stopped. I'm easily deterred. I suspect this is true of mostpeople, certainly of most people in my field. A resistance that doesn't stop *me* needs redefining.

((Whilst no one I've balled—almost—has afterwards resented the sex or myself, and many have come back bearing the same old resistance for more, and a few have even sent friends. And yet most of my victims have offered a specious resistance to my molestations—repeatedly.

(The guideline is the pretense of sleep. I generally ignore the diffuse resistance of sleep, it being unconscious & general, not specifically related to me & what I'm about, but only to one isolate phase of the whole. The sleeper isn't trying to stop me from molesting him, he is only responding to unidentified sensations & pressures. A conscious person consciously seeking to prevent me acts in a much more precise & purposeful fashion, and when that happens I quit.

(Token resistance is a symptom of fake sleep which continues long after the subject can't possibly be still asleep. And this playacting is a consent. The actor & I are playing the same game. If he can easily stop it & does not, he permits it. But this display of resistance shifts all the responsibility on me, so to speak, and soothes the puppy's conscience.

(And the hardon's the contract. Erection implies consent. If you gain the crotch & find a hardon awaiting you, then the boy has clearly long been conscious of what you're doing & why, and where it's heading, and has had a strong physiological reaction to it all—erections are quite honest—and has done nothing to hinder you. (And if, when you reach it, the cock greets you with a glad jump, nobody's fooling anyone.)

(If you encounter a limp cock, this means the boy has truly slept through your preliminaries & sleepeth yet. But if you can arouse the organ to performance level—twitch-state—without being stopped (unless the boy's insanely drunk), a process practically guaranteed to wake the puppy on the way, that too is pretty clear consent.

(We have to go along with these games, of course. The boy is always right, and our object is not to make him uncomfortable or ashamed/guilty or gay—only to make Him. But it furthers one to know that these are games, and how they work.)

When I found Chuck's cock, I found it firm & jumping. Freed it & his netherlands expeditiously, but Chuck wouldn't let his jeans past his knees at first, nor later—when we obviously needed more room—past his ankles, nor would he let me off his shirt, though he gave me free rein under it. This shows a real reluctance, but it also shows consent.

Talk about cocksucking loses interest faster than doing it

does. The details don't vary a hell of a lot, really, save with exceptionally cooperative partners. They're not all alike, but there's only one way to know that. Chuck's was a good cock to suck, and well-mounted, and I gave it my best, even stirring him up so that he switched from passive acceptance to active fucking. He came pleasantly. It was fun. I'd do it again. Then he resumed his garments & lay down & slept. I returned to my desk.

There'd been going around an atrocious oriental flu, marked by sudden onset, a few hours of diarrhea & violent vomiting, followed by 24–48 hours of exhaustion. About an hour after the ball this flu hit Chuck. Bang. He spent the rest of the night in the john, the next two days in my office asleep. No more sex. Shit. And then he left.

Roger Chapuis, 17, Taurus. Found him at Morloch's, where he'd accidentally become wide open to all forms of ambient & directed psychic energy. Brought him to the office & taught him how to handle this energy. This took all night, no sex. Later I kidnapped him from his girlfriend, whisked him to the Riverside house, and took advantage of him in a real bed, as he deserved. Fine-drawn, delicate, fair. Good sex.

He'd hitched from Boston. Had his clothes &c stolen in New Orleans by someone who'd given him a lift: let Roger out of the car & sped off before he c'd grab his luggage.

And a bisexual friend of Allen's (Bob Roter, 21, crew-cut Capricorn just out of jail), a dullish Tarot-freak—good fuck, though.

And a 16-year-old I found hitchhiking at Hywd & Vine one 10 a.m. Induced him to come with me & get high instead, then molested him. Good daytime sex.

And others & others.

My sole marked failure was one Hal Larch, 18, Canadian. He had a sleeping bag. There's no way to get through a sleeping bag that's zipped. Fuck sleeping bags.

All of this activity in about six weeks, during which I put out five issues of *Tuesday's Child*.

Then in January I moved out to Riverside Street in the Valley with Barbara, and my sex life terminated. Four lays in four months, and countless incompleted passes. Almost entirely a defect of geography.

3/4/70 — L.A.

In high school I established by the most rigorous statistical methods that of any five boys I c'd induce to share a bed with me, I c'd count on having sex with three.

I was aware that there were several factors operating to my advantage at the time that were purely temporary. My three out of five & I were the same age, and our age was one at which all kinds of sexual experimentation were normal. The milieu we inhabited was one that encouraged bed-sharing. We all knew each other pretty well, being classmates & all, which made it unlikely that fear w'd be part of their reactions. Nor were my bedmates old enough yet or experienced enough to have established sexual prejudices of any great strength. We were still naive to the point—*I* was, anyhow, at first—of not making the connection between our mutual masturbations & this Sex stuff that people talked about. The two out of five I c'dn't make were generally extreme noli me tangere cases who automatically freaked at having their peters touched, without any thought of sex entering into their panic.

Lee High served a very genteel territory, predominately upper middle class & Protestant, and our innocence-level was abnormally high. Of all my Lee playmates, only Martin Thomas knew what it was all about, and his attempts to escalate the action from cock-rubbing to sucking or buggery freaked me entirely. He kept shoving it at my face, or grabbing my head & shoving my face at it, hissing "Kissss it, kisssss it" & trying to get it into my mouth. I had no idea what this was all about, or why he was doing this, or what he expected of me ("Kiss" to me meant nothing more than bone-dry family lip pats) or meant to do to me. I was scared, and the idea of having someone stick his dirty penis in *my mouth* set me gagging uncontrollably. If I had known what he really wanted to do (*Come?! In MY Mouth!?*) I'd've died. (My mother was a damned effective teacher.)

Oh, if I had only known about fellatio in high school!

Except for Martin Thomas, all my Lee High School j.o. buddies were virgins.

Andrew Jackson, on the other hand, served Jacksonville's white slums, and the level of sophistication was as high as our level of innocence. When I played with Jackson boys, there were only two responses: uninterested rejection or eager & enthusiastic acceptance. No freaking. Jackson boys knew about sex. And they weren't afflicted with middle class morals, either. (Good old Sammy Meyer. Married now, I imagine, with a low-class job, fat & balding like his dad; or, just as likely, in jail.)

But I digress.

I knew that as I grew older I'd lose all these high school advantages, and I expected I wouldn't be balling three out of five much longer.

And I didn't, either. My record's been getting better and better all the time. Nobody gets out of my bed unballed anymore. Almost nobody.

I've been 21 years at this now, and each year's crop of puppies has been less reluctant to ball me than the year before's. Anyone who's willing to share my bed is willing to share his bod. Even Chris Molatin, hysterically opposed to the whole idea, gave me two of the best & most prolonged lays I've ever had. I get most of my sex from kids who need a place to crash—have done since '62 or so, regularly. An endless, self-renewing supply of willing boys. How nice of God to have remembered

6/10/65 — New York

David Dusseldorf, 22, 5'6", redhead, newly come to the East Side from Detroit.

I began my campaign for David a month ago at Wendy's Place on East 11th Street. I took him home then & introduced him to pot, and remain still the only person he knows to get high with. This involved his spending the night with me at the hotel several times.

Using my standard/preferred seduction technique, I failed twice. We never discussed sex, naturally, and now I think I only failed because he didn't understand what I was getting at. The third time, after several fruitless hours of furtive contact, I chanced to tickle the area from anus to testicles, and David responded with unexpected enthusiasm & virtuosity. He introduced me to a new interfemoral technique wherein he was on top, my legs outstretched, his tightly together. My penis fit up between his legs, and his slid tightly between our sweat-slick bellies—my usual position upside down. Remarkably effective: simultaneous orgasms, quite satisfactory.

His body is surprising: hard as stone & perfectly proportioned. Dressed, he just looks skinny.

Afterward was relaxed and easy, with no embarrassment or displeasure. We haven't discussed this since, but David has accepted my invitation to share a pad with me. This bodes amazingly well. Intelligent, young, beautiful, musically gifted, teachable & eager to learn, fun in bed & none of the usual faggoty bullshit—Dave could well be the mythical nice young man to settle down with.

(Much later: we did live together in a basement apartment on East 12th Street for about six weeks, and they were glorious weeks. He was as good to live with as he was to sleep with, and got better at both every day. Gentle, considerate, kind, humorous, sensual—as we moved upon each other he would murmur "Oh pleasure, pleasure." Then someone in his family fell seriously ill & he had to return to Detroit. He said he'd be back in a week or two, and I haven't seen him since. Nor have I heard from him, nor have I any idea what became of him.

(Twelve years have passed, and still I miss you, David.)

9/4/65 — N.Y.

James Montclair, 18, a football player from Pawtucket.

Having missed the last train to Peekskill, I found myself
homeless in Grand Central with five hours to structure, so I
went to a nearby Bickford's & had my daily meal, dexed
beyond reason, and jotted *High Tea* notes as I ate, staring
into space between words to recapture what I was intending
to say. Evidently I was liplicking, twitching & grimacing
somewhat, for at the end of one long stare I found a very
well-designed & packaged crewcut blond youth making faces
at me from across the room—caricatures of sucking, mainly,
dissolving into broad smiles.

This threw me into instant confusion. I was more than
willing, of course, but had no place to take him, and there
was scant chance, considering the neighborhood & time, that
he had a pad handy. And my faith in my dex-warped perceptions & interpretations was, naturally, feeble. I was unsure of
what he had in mind: pleasure, profit, or beating up a fairy.

At last I left Bickford's, very slowly, and loitered outside
in case he wanted to explain himself, but soon I chickened
out & returned to Grand Central. The whole area, as I ought
long ago to have surmised, from Bickford's four blocks south
to 42nd Street, and thence at least the two block length of
the terminal (and doubtless beyond), on both sides of the
street & throughout Grand Central itself, was swarming with
males, mostly straight young goodies, brought together by a
very common interest, and the neighborhood abounds in
cheap hotels, in one of which I hope I remember to establish

myself when I return to the city. Why have I been scuffling in the desert all these years instead of browsing on this bountiful meadow the least twitch of intellect could have located for me?

This abundance of clearly motivated beauties (though none so fine as the face-maker) made sitting still impossible, so I strolled—first back to Bickford's (he was gone), then through Grand Central to 42nd Street eastward, then back again toward Bickford's, rejecting otherwise commendable adventures in hope of finding & salvaging the Bickfordian treasure.

I found him at the Peerless Camera (northeast) corner of 45th & nearly chickened out again. His lavish grin of recognition/invitation seemed heavy with contempt, to which I'm extraordinarily vulnerable.

But I strolled past him & on down 45th the length of two store windows, then pointed my face at some dull camera display & waited for him to join me & strike up a conversation. Being a coward, my object here, as at Bickford's, was to solicit his overt encouragement, without which I dast not proceed.

When it became obvious that this wasn't going to happen, I rounded the grinning corner north for two stores, saying, sotto voce, "I'd love to, but I never learned the rules," as I passed, then came to rest against two of Ma Bell's parked cable spools, stared memory long at the boy-de-vivre. A lovely college boy paused a while to chat, then, unencouraged, passed on.

By now I was excited far beyond the limits of my customary prudence, so I joined him at the corner & drummed up a conversation myself. Luckily, as a result of having taken no sleep, 450 mgs of dex & nine cigarettes per hour since 8 a.m. last Tuesday, my voice was very deep & pleasantly husky.

(My usual high, nasal, diffident light baritone voice helps undermine my confidence when cruising.)

He wasn't as drunk as he let on to be, but drunk enough for jazz, and I was maintaining my own coherence only by heroic efforts of will, or maybe self-deception. (God knows. Preserving my cool when I've got the hots is hard enough straight & rested.) Anyhow, clearing up mutual misunderstandings kept the talk from lagging during the sensitive first few minutes. Then:

"Where's all the cunt at in this town?" he ritually asked.

Busy, I explained, going on to say his question sounded like a classic come-on, one of those statements none of the meaning of which is contained in the words.

"What would you like to do?" a broad hint that he had something to sell.

"You're the cat who's standing on the corner, what would *you* like to do?" seeking to translate the transaction from commerce to service, business to pleasure. I went on to explain, with abnormal candor, that I had never learned the rules, that in my Jacksonville youth I'd learned everything about faggots except just what it was they did, and that by the time I found out what a faggot really was, I had already been one for years & years, wherefore I had not only failed to learn gay rites & procedures in my formative years, but had also grown up with an unquenchable distaste for faggots & faggotry in general, though not, of course, for homophilia. (If anybody else should somehow see these memoranda, note that this was absolutely true.)

As the game had gone on, my confidence had steadily increased, to the point where I was able to deliver yonders autobiographical oddity fluently, with warmth, dry wit & a keen sense of the absurd, in a quietly brilliant spontaneous performance of the sort that made my Village reputation. I hadn't expected that, and I was impressed.

So was he. When his laughter subsided, he exclaimed that he'd never met anyone like me before, and that he really dug me.

Valentine ahead on points.

Then we returned to Topic A, and I said it all depended on whether he was out for pleasure or profit.

Profit, he hinted at some length. This vagueness was encouraging.

That left me out, I said, but if he didn't mind, I'd like to continue the conversation.

He, too.

At this point the game changed from Pickup to New Friends, signalled by his offer of a cigarette. (The precision of these tiny rituals delights my sense of form.)

The talk turned to his difficulties getting a piece of ass: time-hallowed mantalk, signifying the depth of the change in our relationship without ever losing sight of the main subject. He outlined his fleshless adventures on West 45th Street: Pussy Alley.

I told him where that was at, warned him clear of P.R. puta, suggested the Village. I wrote him one each East & West Village list of prime make-out bars & coffee houses, told him what to expect, how to dress & act, and ended with a stimulating lecture on hipchick sexual attitudes, parenthetically explaining why their detachment makes dykes the best whores.

He remarked that it was about time he got to bed, but made no parting move.

So I advised him that the Village chicks he made out with would expect him to smoke pot with them first.

He said he never had but would like to try it.

One of the major train-waiting drags, I told him, was the lack of a safe place to turn on, such a place as, say, his hotel room. Would he like to try pot right now?

Pause.

Yes.

Diabolic.

Off to the Roger Smith Hotel, where first we exchanged addresses, next he angled for & I extended an invitation to visit me this winter (joyfully), and finally my last remaining speck of Panama Red completely destroyed him, to his vast delight.

Then, of course, he invited me to bed.

I'm now seriously tempted to rhapsodize about Jim's amazing body. Instead of the selective overdevelopment I'd expected because of his football training, there was the idealized balance & proportion I simply don't expect in real bodies. A tactile experience of transcendental wealth & subtlety; my hand could feel both the strength that lurked below his fine-grained surface & leapt up to meet the stroking palm, and the prolific life from bone to flesh that sparked the gaps between his luxurious skin & my feather-stroking fingers to outline neural paths & taught me a new & firmer/heavier caress with the butt of the hand across complexities of muscle horse-twitching at my touch.

Fellatio was strenuous, responsive, abandoned, involved, he writhing, legs surrounding me. A dance, by God. And my hands kneading everywhere.

Excitement mounted in a tightening spiral of violent surges, tension, intensity, approaching a deep tremble, until orgasm came in a prolonged electrical vibration that approached rigidity.

Wow.

And then I went back to Grand Central & wrote it all down.

(Jim wrote me several letters that winter, but since I was in Hillside he couldn't visit, not the way we wanted. He admitted that he was really 23, that claiming to be 18 was just commercial window trimming. Finally he was drafted & was never heard of further. I wish you well, Montclair.)

TWO

1967 – 1968

Partially because monomaniacs bore me, partially because effeminate men bug me, partially because of a snobbishness that is actually disguised fear, I've known less than half a dozen other homosexuals at all well, so I've no way to establish how odd or ordinary a specimen I am, and no one to talk with about it, which may be why I take such an almost narcissistic delight in recording & studying the convolutions of my sexuality.

As I get older, the inexorably increasing age differential automatically transforms my status from pederophile to pederast. Like most of my jokes, when, smiling, I call myself a child molester, it's only funny because it's true. (My requirement that the child must consent to being molested—ideally, sh'd initiate the process—is all that saves me from being a leperous moral horror.)

I'm interested in boys, not men. Football players & weight lifters, Clark Gables & Yul Brynners, leave me erotically unconcerned. Youth is the cosmetic that turns male flesh to my obsession. Craggily handsome athletes or body builders, no; but boyish ones can swell my fantasies until I've no spare mind for non-erotic thought & no will but desire to govern me.

Boys. Preferably beautiful boys, but more essentially boys than beauty. Youth is most of my aesthetic. All my life I've known better than to become a teacher.

Given the basic rule, that the boy must consent, fully

knowing what he's consenting to, and the operational requirement that the candidate must be physically capable of playing the game & enjoying it, everything else is pretty much open to negotiation. Acceptable age covers a broad range, for instance. When I was a puppy myself & didn't know what was happening, of course, there were no standards—in the summer of '47 (I think) in Dallas, I cheerfully allowed myself to be repeatedly seduced by a nine-year-old who'd been corrupted in San Diego, unthinkable now—but since leaving high school the range has been from puberty to around (but very youthful) 35. Aside from my youngest puppy, a precocious 12-year-old pool lounger (son of a friend of the boss) at the Travellers Motel who was already a two-year carnal veteran, and the jocularly horny 14-year-old son of a guest at the motel, the spring-flesh meadow I've browsed upon has been unfailingly graced with pubic hair. Within this age range, the younger, generally, the better. A flawless 21-year-old can retroactively shade a whole week with anticipation, a 17-year-old can restore my faith in nameless wonders I've not known I'd lost faith in, gold vibrating in my memory, while a 15-year-old w'd constitute a major health hazard.

I like (but don't demand) a beauty of face that escapes definition, in that it includes not only what is usually thought of as beauty, but also much that w'd generally be called plain, and some of what most people w'd consider ugly. Aside from traditional beauty (which is generally acceptable even when it's as passively immobile as plastic or sullen as self-indulgent boredom), liveliness, I think, is the determining factor—liveliness & humor. Almost all lively, expressive faces are beautiful.

I like (but also don't demand) good physical development —adolescent statuary—rather firmly soft than exceedingly hard, but I also like skinniness. Only fat do I reject. A perfectly proportioned puppy is a luxury rare enough to merit asterisks & other exceptional indices in my record, but I do not sleep alone solely for lack of such, and there are other qualifications that take precedence over perfect proportion.

I like but almost never encounter & even less often take to bed a lushly velvety complexion, seemingly translucent & lit from within (you've seen such), but neither acne nor acne scars serve to disqualify an otherwise acceptable puppy.

I'm fond of intelligence, but only for extended engagements is it necessary. For an evening's entertainment, the puppy needn't necessarily have a mind at all, as long as the rest of his equipment is present & functional. The very few retarded puppies I've bedded far more than made up in action for their conversational deficiencies.

I like hair. The current crop of long-haired puppies has been an unexpected treasure for me. Red hair touches some chord in me that vibrates more loudly than commonsense. Baldness turns me off.

On & on & on. I pretty much insist on heterosexual—or at least non-swishy—puppies. I seek perfection but settle for less. I prefer healthy puppies. All my tastes were established by my high school experiences & yearnings. Today's puppies reflect '47-'50 Jacksonville prototypes.

There are distinct advantages to pederasty. One is that there's a new crop of puppies every year, but the greatest is that the world is so designed that pederasts are balanced by sodomites—puppies who dig older men. (Of all these technical terms I'm somewhat doubtful. I mean them to mean what I say they mean: be advised.) This is the basis of the traditional teacher/student relationship, of the classic Greek bit, &c. This was the structure of my scene with Allen Pierce, long-loved & lost, with anyone I've lived with rather than just balled. And

due to the damage done to the paternal image/status in
America since the war, there's a mild sodomy explosion going
on currently, a growing surplus of goodies for a relatively
stable dirty-old-man population. I expect in L.A. to acquire
at least a beddable writer's apprentice, if not a full harem.

This journal begins thus in the gutter mainly because I've
been growing horns uninterruptedly since June 8th, have for
the past two months been futilely staring at daily brigades of
beautiful Hollywood high school boys, and am now—self-
confidence & finances simultaneously restored—waiting for
an overdue Greyhound to take me to Miami, there to check
into the Y, where the ground rules are all known, hopefully
to end my drought of flesh.

There turns out to be no vacancy at the Y, and thus I'm
deprived of the classical simplicity of operation I was counting on. Now, instead of finding neatly naked puppies in the
shower waiting or supine in darkened rooms with open doors,
inviting towel-draped guests in from the hall—instead of that
so convenient unequivocal singleness of purpose—I've got to
go out into the city, hunt puppies like a sportsman hunting
deer, establish clear relationships & determine the name of
the game, and lure them into my room past a desk clerk of as
yet unknown prejudices—a far more strenuous undertaking
than I'd counted on & more susceptible to failure, and if I *do*
score there'll probably be a price tag. Ai-yah.

On the basis solely of having escorted to it a few months
ago a lost & confused puppy who was too drunk to find his
way back alone, and also too drunk even for consideration &
approach, let alone balling, I've taken for two nights ($14)
room 306 at the Hotel Belfort, about which I know in total
nothing. The room has a double bed, a desk, a bath, a sink &

a lockable door—not luxurious, but adequate for my purposes.

And now it's 8 o'clock & I'm off. Luck & lust.

To complicate things needlessly further, it's raining. Also, this hotel seems to be devoted to old folks & drunks. I'm sorely tempted to rent yet another room—in the hotel two lots west of here, the lobby of which was rich in puppies when I passed an hour ago—and cruise from two bases. Or maybe I sh'd barhop? No, not until 0100 or thereabouts, when the mere tourists & other dross have extracted themselves, leaving the hungry loners in command of the field.

This neighborhood is highly Cubanized. That adds yet another element of uncertainty to my quest. Unfamilar mores, conventions, traditions, signals, games & prizes. Unfamiliar people whom I do not understand. Gaudy excesses of doubt.

Damn. Getting laid shouldn't be this much work. I'll be glad to get back west where things are simpler.

And now I'm additionally established for one experimental night ($5.15) in room 205 of the Strand Hotel, and my two hotel rooms command views of each other. This is more of a dump than the Belfort, but it too has a private bath. There are times when a communal bathroom is most desirable. How else does one meet people in a strange city?

But the rain has stopped. If I can smuggle a puppy in past either of the desk clerks, I may yet accomplish my objective. If so, I'll return perhaps to Hollywood tomorrow.

Tomorrow I've got to see about transportation to L.A.

If I don't score tonight, I'll continue the quest, as usual, into the daylight hours, barring cloudburst.

10/10/67 — Miami

Except, of course, that it isn't daylight at all, it's rainlight. It w'd begin to seem that I'm doomed again.

10/16/67 — Hollywood

Drought broken accidentally by one Chuck O'Donnell (blond, bella figura, my height, 21-25), who pulled up in a panel truck in downtown Hywd where I'd been having coffee & doughnuts & offered me a ride anywhere round about midnight.

Turned out to be my first go at an experienced & fully developed straight male under the ordinary circumstances—fellatio exclusively, his terms, &c—in over two years (it's usually me in charge) and I was at a severe disadvantage. Especially as he really digs sex & balled over an hour nonstop before coming, causing me something like lockjaw from long lack of exercise, and asphyxiation from my Florida sinuses. Nevertheless I gave full satisfaction, and was fully satisfied. Afterwards he praised my performance. Praise I like.

However, just before leaving he asked for $2. Fool that I am, I gave him $5, and he saw a $10 in my wallet, plus a few $1s, and took those too. (I'm not about to argue about money with someone in that physical condition.) I persuaded him to give a dollar back for cigarettes, and didn't mention the $500 in my desk drawer.

I imagine I'll learn, but I can't imagine when.

Still, this was less than several futilities here in Southern Florida have cost me, and it's nice to get something for the money for a change. Each gave the other what he wanted: fair trade. My feeling I've been had's unjustified.

Later:

This morning, my final Hollywood street dawn, a few of the local longhairs thawed at last & were friendly & conversation-prone. We talked a while at a coffeeshop, then walked a while watching tadpoles skoot to school. Then we parted.

We didn't talk about much—standard head shoptalk—and I don't recall any names, nor they mine, I suppose—but had so much as this happened in August or September, I might not now be leaving for L.A.

So hostile this place has been, these people. So shouting out car windows at my hair, my beard, never speaking. Say good morning, anyone is scared. Amazing.

I say again, I am a trivial man, in need of frequent renewal. New ideas, new minds, new faces, bodies, new locales, in that order, make me new.

Every day we make the whole world new.

Or else grow old.

Generally, big men are easier to make & safer to solicit than
little men. Short men are more uptight about their manliness
than tall ones, and (a) tend to regard homosexual approaches
as threats to it, or slights upon it (even though my approaches
& projects are testimonials to their masculinity), and (b) tend
to regard their pussy track records as prima facie evidence of
their supernal maleness and consequently to be obsessive in
their cunt chasing, thus leaving me no openings & no time to
cultivate openings. Tall men, on the other hand, are more
relaxed about all this, and are ready to consider a proffered
blowjob simply as sex.

    In Miami once I spent almost a month trying to seduce a
pretty midget who habitually wore a cowboy suit, looking
tough. I think my motive was mainly bizarre curiosity. I'd
never balled a midget, and the idea per se appealed to me—like
fucking a doll. But this midget was put off by the idea of
balling me. I didn't understand this. My thinking was that,
his opportunities for normal sex being so obviously limited,
he'd welcome the chance to have sex at all. Wrong. I have yet
to fuck a midget—or be fucked *by* one, which is more to the
point. As during the course of the month my advances evolved
from subtle toward gross, his rejections evolved to match, till
at the end I was making loud noises & he was so convincingly
pretending I wasn't there I was coming to believe him. That's
when I gave it up.

The basic operations of homosexual love, like those of hetero-sexual love, are few—four, in fact—but ample.

Simplest is masturbation. Mutual masturbation has been many a young boy's introduction to sex. It's a friendly and even affectionate way, but somewhat impersonal, with little scope for passion. Sophistications are on the order of, say, moistening the hands. (You can also, of course, make use of strange things & substances. A young neo-Nazi I knew 20 years ago in New York had a cigar box with a cock-sized hole in it, which he would fill with liver & fuck. A friend of mine masturbates in stockings—I'm told this is very common.) Great subtlety is possible, but rare.

Face-to-face intercourse is accomplished in three general ways:

A. The Princeton Rub

The participants lie close-pressed, tete-a-tete, either on their sides or one atop the other, cocks up & rubbing against their bellies. This is especially effective in warm weather when sweat makes the pressed-together bellies wet, slick & cuntlike. The only real drawbacks are (1) the difficulty of keeping the cocks in place (they tend to slip to one side, out of contact, and must be speedily reposi-tioned by hands that c'd be better employed elsewhere), and (2) the gooey wet smear of come widespread over both bellies when it's over, which can be inconvenient.

B. The Interfemoral Cunt

Lying face to face as above, the active partner places his penis between the other's thighs, the receptive partner's penis being as in A above (with attendant disadvantages). The receptive partner presses his thighs together to form a pretty fair imitation cunt. Lubrication—spit or sweat, generally—helps. The only disadvantage, besides those of A above, is that a pool of come collects on the sheets, making them wet & uncomfortable to sleep on afterwards.

(A & B above are my own preferred fucks.)

C. The Anal Approach

The receptive partner, lying on his back with a pillow under his arse to prop it up, raises his legs as high as he can, much as though he were performing the calisthenic rite called 'riding the bicycle,' and spreads them wide enough for his friend to get between. The active partner then inserts his cock in receptive's anus, which, in this leg position, is fairly wide open, as such things go. Receptive wraps his legs not too tightly around active, as any girl w'd any boy, and they do fuck, as any girl & boy w'd.

It is helpful if the active partner be somewhat taller than the passive, so that their faces can meet despite the fact that, at the other end, they're an arse-length apart.

Lubrication is almost mandatory. K-Y lubricating jelly, Vaseline, cold cream, Wildroot hair cream, butter, spit—I've used them all, and now there are specifically sexual lubricants on the market.

The receptive partner must be able to voluntarily relax his anal sphincter, or there will be pain. But this is easy to do (and the active partner can help by judicious finger-in-rectum foreplay), once you get the idea, and even so, the pain is brief. The initial penetration may hurt if you're not relaxed & ready, but the withdrawal eases the pain, and the next thrust hurts less, if at all. By the 3rd or 4th thrust & withdrawal, usually, all pain is gone, replaced by pleasure. (Getting fucked in the arse feels Good.) (Drunkenness is a great aid to relaxation.)

More commonly, anal intercourse is performed with the active partner entering from the rear. Thus: receptive lying face down, legs apart, with a pillow under his belly to elevate the anus for easy access. The active partner inserts his cock & lies at full length on the passive's back, hugging him and fucking joyfully.

Or both lie on their sides, the passive partner drawing his legs up as though squatting, to make his arsehole open & easily entered. Penetration is shallower in this position than in the others, generally. (Naturally, once penetration has been accomplished, the squatting attitude of the passive's legs is no longer necessary, and he can do with them as he pleases.)

Or receptive on hands & knees, active mounting doggie style. After penetration has been established, this position may be maintained, or it may flow into the full-length position, or even into the side position. All of these positions tend to merge into one another.

(An odd variant: active partner lies on his back, cock raised like a spike. Passive partner squats over the spike and impales himself on it, and then slides up & down on it. I was cast in this active role in the Miami YMCA once, and it really blew my mind.)

I'm tempted to write an essay on arse fucking . . . but not now.

In the face-to-face methods, both parties commonly experience orgasm, fairly often together (this can be cultivated). In the rear-entry anal methods, unless it's a trade affair with the active partner maintaining his straight purity, the active partner generally masturbates the passive whilst fucking him. Even without this helping hand, the passive partner will often enough achieve orgasm anyway from the massaging effect of his friend's cock on his prostate.

Fellatio is the fourth basic operation. The secret of fellatio is that a mouth is more versatile than a cunt. Fellatio sh'd be performed with the utmost sensuality, and a good blow job sh'd take a longish time, with the active partner moaning & saying Oh God & the like all the while.

In the usual casual blow job, the active partner lies inert whilst the receptive does all the work. This is foolish, for it robs the active partner of most of the pleasure he c'd be getting from the act. If, instead, he sh'd cooperate & properly fuck the mouth that's sucking him, he'll find fellatio to be one of the finest sexways available.

In the standard American blowjob, only the active partner comes. This is an artistic defect.

The alternative—the famous 69—avoids this defect, but is not, to my mind, the very best sex. There is an impersonal quality to it, compared to the tete-a-tete and anal forms. I'm interested in more of my partner than just his cock. Also (this is a technical weakness of mine) I find it hard to give proper attention simultaneously to both sucking & being sucked. And 69 is the least fuck-like of all the methods I've outlined. However, I'll never turn down an invitation to 69 from anyone I'm willing to go to bed with at all.

That is to say, "I've had good & I've had bad, and the worst I've had was Wonderful."

These idle thoughts generated by the sound of Eric Descartes & Amelia balling grandly in the next room for six action-packed hours, the last of which devoted to what sounded like a masterly giving of head by La Kidd. I wouldn't mind giving Eric head—or anything else—myself, but don't look for it to happen.

8/24/70 — L.A.

Bronson Park Cave—
    "I don't know 'bout you, man, but I'm here to get laid."
    "? What do you have in mind?"
    "You give head?"
    "Sometimes."
    "Look! I already got a hard on."
    "So you do."
    Grope. Clinch. Unwrapping. Short, competent fellatio.
    Moans & squirms. Hands grip head. Tastes good, as such things go.
    "Yeah."
    And again inside, lying on the sand. He gropes & jerks off in harmony. Significant. Later:
    "See you."
    "Peace."
    Hot afternoon.

Puppies spend more time naked than they did when I was one, and more time in conducive situations. Had I this here/ now to grow up in, I'd've grown up stranger than I am.

WANTED: Live-in boy. Will teach Magick in return for company and certain liberties.

10/14/69 — L.A.

So Balzak ran off in June, and when I asked the Ching "Now what?" she told me Grace.

Grace? By July 1 I'd taken up Magick to console myself, and started hanging around The Compleat Enchanter, an occult magic store in a psychedelic supermarket at the corner of Hywd Blvd & Las Palmas, across the street from the notorious Blue Fish coffeeshop: heart & hub of the puppyhustler industry in Los Angeles. Oh! such acres of young shirtlessness, such blond & tanned, so flesh & many! Oh!

I touched as many of them as I could without creating an accurate but useless impression & name for myself. All backs & shoulders, almost, are fair game & officially manly. Under ideally crowded or quietly staged conditions, fleeting buttock contact is possible. Certain naturally affectionate pups, or especially friendly open types, are good for prolonged back & shoulder parking.

At home I found myself masturbating more often than has/had been my wont.

The whole trouble was that Endor Park & home were so impossibly distant from Hywd & Las Palmas. If there'd been any way to get them home, I could've fondled my fill of lush puppies—homeless ones, horny ones, curious ones, innocent ones, unsuspecting ones, eager & willing ones, all kinds & colors. Even with a gay hangout across the street, there was a puppy glut. But I lived eight miles away, the puppies lived even farther off or nowhere, and we none of us had cars.

Even if the crop'd been leaner, I had money at the time & could've bought me a playmate from the horde of hustlers on the corner, most of whom surpassed my aesthetic requirements. But not without a place to go.

July 7th I was two weeks into this festival of frustration, and along came John Carlsson. He was a 14-year-old blond little Taurus talking a worldly-wise & sexually-liberated line, by his own testimony an unrestrainedly horny & lascivious youngling, who rejoiced in unparalleled freedom from parental supervision & rules, his very own man at just 14, who did offer to journey with me to Siberia to be taught the mysteries of the Ching.

His kind of 14 was nearly too young, though he was adequately cocked for his own purposes. Also his face lived in a blond limbo of neither pretty nor not-pretty, and he was short enough to pass for 12, and still wore most of his baby fat.

Yet I am at root a child molester of sorts. I've had joy of a 12-year-old, and a 14-year-old as well, in Miami Beach during my Travellers Motel days, though not since, and I'm generally still willing to take on any reasonably attractive puplet who offers himself. Besides, small John was the first male to've put himself in my clutches since Balzak evaporated.

Long evening bus ride to Endor Park & Sunset. Very Very Very long wait there for the Endor Park bus, I babbling my best to keep John unbored & still willing. Boys so nearly children can be wayward & quick-changeable, short on patience & sullen in the absence of action. Nevertheless the bus eventually came.

Home, I broke out my dwindling stash & we started Chingtalk. My object was to get John superstoned & sleepish.

In come loudly Teddy & Katje. Katje's a female Dutch

artist friend of my next door neighbor Marc's, she 40-ish & flighty. Teddy is her paramour, skinny southern blond, 27, recently pretty but now gone to blear. He means to strike it rich as a rock star—singing. But wilted.

Katje's got a problem. Teddy has a bottle of wine. Katje's had a spell laid on her by an examoratus. Teddy's drunk. I tell her what to do about it. Teddy spills his wine.

(All the while I'm carefully not offering them any grass. There's barely enough left for the Johnny project.)

Teddy's cut a demo record & is overconfident it'll get him a recording contract. Not bloody likely, I thinks. He spots Ching paraphernalia & insists on throwing a change on said contract. Spills more wine doing so. Youthful Folly changing to The Army. Right on.

Katje's turn. Approach, changing to Peace.

I eventually tell them they're encroaching on my teaching time. They get the hint slowly & sulkily leave. Teddy forgets his bottle. He'll never miss it.

So John & I go back to Chingchat, smoke grass, swill vinegar wine. Turns out this boy's no lasting treasure. He's dull, incurious, assertive & a bore. Knows no thing but self & friends. It's not fair to judge him on this—what more can you expect of a 14-year-old in adult company? (Plenty.) But he's still no unalloyed delight, and I'm glad he's a transient.

Comes fallout time at last. Only token resistance to sharing a bed. Peace.

Now I play again that waiting I learned two years older than he. Waiting for him to sleep. Making sure. Waiting more. Repeatedly, just when I'm 4/5ths sure he's sleeping, his wide-awake voice finds a question to ask. And we wait. The plan—same old plan—calls for fait accompli. Get things started in his sleep, so that he wakens gradually to a scene he's unconsciously accepted before becoming aware of it. My statistics show that most puppies will not try to stop a party if they've already got an erection in my hand when first they notice it.

When he's asleep beyond question, I slowly pounce. Instead of the old flank attack, approaching Mt. Penis by infinitesimal increments up the hip & across the thigh, imperceptibly advancing on my goal like a horny glacier, with perverse delight in the prolongation of the process & paranoid care not to disturb the proprietor—instead of this I let my hand, like a helicopter, settle so gently down right on top of his wee little thing.

I wonder if the 30-yr-old woman he claims to've balled knew that's what he was doing?

Stroke & rub & press the head &. This calls for great precision. Squeeze the head & rub & stroke &.

He gets it up finally. It isn't very impressive, but it's there, and a great improvement over what I've been getting since Balzac. Any perverse pleasure I might have taken in his extreme youth was foiled & flawed & cancelled by his endless talking earlier, but now: 'hello, wee peter. Wanna play?'

(I'm a touch-freak. When I've a cock in hand, I've already attained a major goal. Anything beyond that's gravy.)

"I don't do that any more," John wakes, rolling over on his side, away from me.

"Sorry." I'm almost relieved. I return to my pillow to call it a night.

John, however, decides he wants to split & visit the friends he's been talking about all night. I explain that it's 0400 & there's no transportation.

He says he'll hitch. Gets up, dresses, splits.

There must be better ways to pass the time.

Next I take aim at Chris Molatin, 19, Taurus, incredible, whom I'd found at a Tarot class at the Enchanter. This is a boy of unholy beauty. Enormous blue eyes ringed all around with thick dark lashes like a 1920's belle. Tall, exceptionally broad-shouldered & narrow hipped, slim—maybe 3½-4 inches through at the navel. For this I don't need to be desperate.

He's been over once & we've talked long & earnestly about the magical family 31 & I are thinking of forming, and related short subjects, and about him & me, singly & as room-mates. A most tentative (God! he's beautiful!) seduction attempt has been detected & averted. Chris doesn't go for such things. They scare him.

So I resort to Magick.

That night (he having gone home) I write his name on an index card. Then I erect a magic (*I Ching*) circle on the vanity at the foot of my bed and place Chris's name at the center of the circle. The same circle has been drawn on the large round mirror of the vanity, and Chris's circle is reflected in it. Naked I get in bed & lo! I too am reflected in the circle on the mirror.

Now I masturbate diligently whilst elaborating a powerful fantasy upon Chris. I pay far more attention to the sensual aspects of masturbation than usual, draw what's generally a 3-minute gesture of defeat out to half an hour or more of nearly good sex—maintaining the fantasy all the while, keeping it & my hand action perfectly coordinated, letting my hand be Christopher, moaning his name—until finally we come together, he in fantasy & I in buckets. Whereat I do smear my semen upon Chris's name in the middle of the circle, stating my will in simple terms, and sit back to see what happens.

Next day comes Chris again to visit, bearing with him LSD. Very hot July day.

We drop the acid & sit around in my livingroom talking about Magick &c. We sit on the floor, crosslegged, close, facing each other, staring into each other's eyes intensely. Chris hath a mystical Thing about communication.

We put our forearms over each other's shoulders, leaning toward each other. Then our heads, the tops of our heads, are touching, holding each other up. And my hands are moving slow & rivery down & airy up his half acre of back, and his on mine.

We fall slowly over on our sides to the floor & lock into embrace & kiss. His tongue is surprisingly soft & unmuscular, but his cock is proud, and he thrusts his leg between my legs and we flow even closer together. This goes on for some time, incredible.

Then we break for air. I suggest a more appropriate costume, Chris a more fitting place. We shed our clothes & explode into bed.

We are locked together, mouth to mouth, belly to belly, groin to groin, the greatest degree of physical contact possible with our anatomies, and we stay locked, moving together like tides, like sliding halves of a single device, at least three hours in that afternoon heat & sunglare. We sweat together, lubricating the contact area, sliding freely like well-oiled pistons, never breaking contact, never lessening it, all those hours.

And we do come from the moment we hit the bed uninterruptedly the whole time, constant orgasm, the room reeking of rich come, the sheet squishing, without pause or abatement.

And we say things. Astonished expressions of love. Proclaiming each other Beautiful. Short sentences. He says we've done this before and I know we have. When I open my eyes what I see is too bright & too wonderful & closes them again, but what I see is Egypt of the Gods, and Christopher & I are making the seasons. The Sun and the Earth making love and the seasons.

Three solid hours!

It was the first mystical/religious/occult lay I'd ever had, a thing I'd always known to be impossible. Transcendental ecstacy. Sacramental. Mythic. We really were making the seasons. We came together and were the summer sun & earth. Unheard of. The mystical union et cetera. Like Kether balling Chokmah.

After completion we went next door to (absent) Marc's and showered together. Here insert lyric poem to Christopher's weird & beautiful body, too wide & too thin, and all velvet & silk. Then we fell onto Marc's bed and did it some more, but not the same and not for long.

There followed a long scene of Christopher's stomach threatening to erupt, I trying to placate it with yogurt & failing, and Chris barfing green & misery into Marc's aseptic kitchen sink. (Later I learned he does that every time he takes acid, but at the time I was sore dismayed.)

He stayed that night, but slept on the livingroom couch. (Oh! I remember. It was on a Sunday, and he had just that morning moved in, bag & book box, to be my roommate. The acid, furthermore, which he requested, was provided by me, copped (stolen) from Marc. Memory strikes again.)

Next day we talked at great length and to little avail. Chris complained that my speech, my mode of expression &c, was dishonest in some way he never made clear, though we spent some hours trying. Also (or maybe only) insincere. No. Honesty was part of it.

Then we went to Libbi's, met a witch there called Hetta who bothered him a lot, went home.

Now his burden was that Libbi & I were both insincere, and that we played head games (I had subtly baited Hetta) and were in general unworthy of the regard he'd had for us (or me anyhow: I think that was his first exposure to Libbi). He used the word 'Communication' a lot. Also used exclusively astrological examples to back his thesis.

And then he repacked bookbox & bag in his car & moved back out.

I didn't know what to make of all this. It didn't hold together no matter how I viewed it. Finally I decided to accept it as itself, an exceptional experience all around. But I deactivated the spell I'd cast and vowed never to work that kind of sex magic again. Later Libbi told me it had been a quite black magic.

(And much later I realized that much of Chris's upset was caused by his natural inability to understand how he had come to do such a thing, so opposed to all his will & ways, so foreign to him, so—to him—distasteful . . . how he'd come to do it and, worse, to enjoy it. Imagine the conflict our season-making must have set up in him. God, I'm sorry.

(He quite justly felt I was responsible, though how & for what he couldn't understand. He didn't know about the spell, but he accurately sensed a dishonesty. Ai-yah.

(Be advised: sex magic yields nothing more than sex, nothing good anyhow, certainly nothing else as good. It makes for good sex but sour love.

(It isn't worth it.)

3/12/68 — L.A.

Ray Downey, 25, counterman at nearby Cooper's Donuts. A fetching youth, well assembled, tall & slim & broad, brown eyes & brown-gold hair. Smells good—doughnuts & coffee, most likely, admixt with Ray.

I encountered him first on a coffee run Sunday night, and, naturally, lusted for him on sight. And lo! Monday night he invites himself to my pad to turn on—i.e., smoke his one & only joint—and then crash.

This provided me with a nearly ideal re-creation of my old high school "tacit agreement" technique.

Also Monday night I scored 200 bennies for $10—a bargain price (50% off) thanks to Libbi & Jim, but my last $10. The thing to do now is use those pills to make money—writing &c. Right.

3/13/68

"Gene," a short, boyish, reddish-haired kid (age still unknown) whom I plucked almost bodily from a bus stop bench at Santa Monica & Vermont at 0230 hours. He'd just arrived by thumb from Denver & asked me if I knew where he c'd rent a room for the night cheap—under $4—whereupon I dutifully invited him to crash with me.

This "cheap room for the night" line seems to be a standard code hereabouts. Ray used the same line last night. It means, "If you let me crash with you, I'll go along with anything that may chance to transpire." A blunt offer to pay rent in flesh.

Nothing w'd do for Gene but to be blown. However, near the base of his cock were a few rough scabs from having been kicked there in a recent fight. (One certainly hopes so.) These rendered said cock inaesthetic, reducing markedly my enjoyment thereof, so I gave him a pretty perfunctory blow.

Ray turns out to be a devout homosexual (it certainly doesn't show). This afternoon he spoke most freely to Marc & me, whilst I was making ready for the Les Crane Show. Seems he has a problem with a lovely & submissive 19-year-old puppy acid freak not unlike my problems in S.F. with Allen.

Ray & Marc & I are apparently becoming, in record time, a circle. Thus: Ray skipped work last night to come to the show, and afterward he went home with Marc. We've actually talked in terms of a mushroom expedition to Mexico. (Ray knows Mexico well—30 plus trips—and speaks translator-class Spanish).

5/1/68

Merlin, 18-year-old Air Force brat, recent ex-square now turned hippy & in a hurry to experience everything. Encountered at Libbi & Jim's, where I'd brought Ray Downey to visit. The evening featured a lot of nudity—Jim, Ray, Merlin, Libbi: almost distressing. The subject of homosexuality was roundly discussed, mostly by Ray.

This discussion apparently set Merlin up for me. At 0500 he & I split to my pad where we blew some hash & UV-treated grass. Eventually I said, "I brought you over here firmly intending to make a pass, but now that I've got you here I can't figure out the proper way to go about it."

He replied that he'd come with me for just that purpose, that he was completely ignorant—like a 15-year-old chick the first time, his image—and that I sh'd take charge. So I did.

(This is the sort of sunrise dialogue I like best. May it happen often is the earnest prayer of the undersigned John Valentine.)

We played a game of constantly shifting roles, just the thing to titillate a would-be decadent eighteener without either conforming to or unduly upsetting his preconceptions. I undressed him slowly & in loving detail, unveiling inch by inch the chunky blond loveliness that had so distressed me at Libbi & Jim's. All this leisurely foreplay was pure luxury, absolutely unnecessary. He was excited—erect—from the moment I first touched him. By the time my questing had arrived at his crotch, it felt as though he had a leaping rock pent in his levi's, and when, with his help, I mastered the engineering of his belt buckle & lowered the zipper, his cock leapt forth like the jack of a jack in the box, eager & ready.

(A pause here to mourn the hip abandonment of underwear. There are few pleasures greater than unpeeling a horny boy like an erotic onion, and the joy of reducing everything to a pair of shorts with a lump inside, then to delay, rubbing the lump, easing fingers under the elastic for fleeting fleshly contacts until the fabric of the shorts is taut to bursting, then the joyful cooperative hump of hips as the shorts are slid down the silky columns of legs to expose the happy cock pressed tight against the belly—all this is lost in a mere shift of whim. Bring back underwear! sh'd be my battle cry.)

Merlin, be advised, hath blond pubic hair. Very rare,

especially among blonds. But Merlin's a wiry, kinky, sandy blond, the kind that often have blond pubic hair, and are often hairy all over. Merlin's not hairy. Head hair (long), a shadow on his upper lip that'll probably remain a shadow five more years, two pale tufts in armpits, very lightly fuzzy (really smooth) arms & long legs, the hairfield of his crotch with a thin line questing upward (hidden now by his tumescence) toward the navel, all utterly pleasing, and otherwise quite hairless. A boy-statue carved out of flesh.

As I undress him, he undresses me. As I touch him, he touches me. Naked at last & tightly hugging, we move together in that slow & ancient dance all other dances merely echo, fucking standing up. I tickle his buttocks—he didn't know they were ticklish—and he thrusts against me with sudden vigor, unbalancing us.

We fall upon my handy bed and fuck forever, face to face, cock to cock between our bellies rubbing, dry at first but ever more & more lubricated by glad sweat. This is what I'd planned, it being, of all homosexual devices, the one least extraneously upsetting for beginners.

We breathe heavily, panting parts of words & grunting, ohing & ahing gloriously, our hands all over each other finding centers of sensation, while the sensations in our cocks (mine, anyway, and from the evidence, his) mount ever in electrical intensity until explosively we come, spurting hot goo across our sweat-slimed stomachs—the spunky, almost Clorox smell of semen set at liberty—and fuck beyond that to exhaustion & lie still.

"Oh wow," says Merlin, and "Oh wow! That was great!" and falls asleep.

We woke around noon, still face to face, cemented together by dried come. We separated carefully and headed for the shower. We showered together in the narrow stall—a boy-like thing, redolent of P.E.—as intimately touching, perforce, as we'd been in bed.

As we soaped & washed each other, our cocks arose again. We were playful, duelling cock to cock, comparing lengths, rubbing & tweaking, exciting each other all over again.

Out of the shower & barely dry, we fell into my bed again. This time, not having to worry about shocking a virgin, I went down on him & started out a long & pyrotechnic blow. So Merlin shocked me by squirming around & going down on me. Like last night, he did everything to me I did to him, and the results were wholly satisfactory. I came shortly before he did, and Merlin swallowed my semen without gagging, then came himself with lots of squish & charming sound effects.

We turned again to face each other. Merlin licked his lips & said "Tastes good," waking echoes in my head from 1943. Truly a remarkable boy.

We dried each other off, got dressed, and headed back to Libbi & Jim's. There we found the very same people we'd left at five ayem. They applauded us roundly as we entered & demanded that we tell them all about it. I was, as always, tongue-tied, but Merlin obliged in detail. When he finished there was more applause & a general kissing of us both.

I'm as fond of a glorious fuck as anyone, but the publicity afterwards was just a bit too much.

5/10/68

The situation at Libbi & Jim's, outlined 5/1 above, lasted, minus Merlin (damn), through 5/8. Libbi & Jim, Sammy Lamont, Ray Downey & myself, all wired on my dexedrine, endlessly discussing, analyzing, Ray's sexual & other hangups in that small, over-heated, piss-scented & baby-dominated furnished hovel.

The first day I cured Ray's psychic impotence by insight & word magic, talking him into it, through it & out. The cure was soon verified by little Sammy.

This was in itself psychically draining, but it got worse. The gift of Merlin's absolutely virgin body, appreciated & cultivated though it was, was not repeated, but the sole topic of talk remained sex—the love life of a chicken queen (Ray) exhaustively explored. Further, little Sammy engaged in marathon sexplay with Libbi & Ray, but not J. Valentine, the whole time. All of which soon became repetitious & boring, and frustrating as hell.

Eventually I went home & recreated Merlin in my hand.

12/12/68 — N.Y.

Hexagram 56, The Wanderer, continues to be my sign. When I arrived in the City, I checked in as a temporary expedient (not without some erotic ulteriority) at the McBurney YMCA. There I met one Steve Roper, a 19-year-old from Oklahoma City, operating the elevator—a nice-seeming kid, skinnily pretty—and struck up a friendship with him. (This was in July. I've been too busy to write.)

Through John Camden I got in touch with Bessie. She was about to move to San Francisco and offered me her $35-a-month pad—previously Bob Nolan's—at 122 Ridge Street, below Houston Street in the very lowest part of the Lower East Side.

Of course I accepted, and, with patently impure motives, invited Roper, who was living at Sloane House, to share the place with me. My intention was, as usual, to carnally molest the youth as gently but thoroughly as opportunity allowed. Never laid a finger on 'im, but I understand better now the importance of intentions.

We moved in on August 1. Very soon thereafter, Steve offered an acquaintance of his shelter at our place, quite unbeknownst to me. The friend, a small, effete quadroon, elected to share the bed with me—Roper coyly occupied the livingroom couch throughout—and instead of my molesting young Roper, I found myself being molested by his friend, whose name I didn't know & whose face I had not yet even seen.

Very educational, thus to have one's customary tables

turned on one. Educational but not especially enjoyable. I don't suppose I'd mind being molested by someone I myself would like to molest, but Roper's friend, like all effeminate homosexuals, turned me off entirely, and I barely managed to avoid being mushily raped. Now I understand my own victims rather more than I would like to, and take care to limit my activity to youths who impress me as being willing. My career as a gentle rapist is, if not altogether terminated, at least considerably abridged.

Realizing that Roper had outdone me all around, and not wanting to share my bed night after night with an unappetizing queen & my pad with an inaccessible puppy, I moved with as much of my belongings as I could comfortably carry, about ½, to the good old Hotel Winston on West 8th Street, scene of many a previous happy ball.

A week later I returned to the Ridge St. pad & found Roper, his buddy, and the balance of my possessions—including some looseleaf notebooks from San Francisco, my typewriter & my alto recorder—gone gone gone. In an atypical fit of energetic fury I destroyed the apartment—never did that before, don't expect to do it again—and went out hunting for Roper & retribution.

He turned out to be still running the elevator on the midnight to 8 shift at the McBurney Y. He seemed effusively glad to see me. He'd been worried, he said. The landlord at 122 Ridge had shown up demanding two months' rent (Bessie'd deceived me) or immediate departure, said Roper. So he'd moved, along with my belongings, to the apartment of yet another friend—a tall, thin, pretty 19-year-old Oklahoman need never lack for friends in New York City—where all my things were safe & waiting to be returned to me. This was good to hear. Steve offered to deliver my goodies to the office that next afternoon. I said groovy, and we parted on the very best of terms.

I never saw him again. He didn't deliver my chattels to the office. He quit his elevator job. He vanished.

Thus have I at last been penalized for impurity of motive. I am chastened, taught, and pissed.

The Winston has declined remarkably since '63. New owner, a hard-faced, shrill old woman rich in evil, possibly a witch, and new clientele & conditions to match. Puerto Rican drag queens, prostitutes, hustlers, pimps, assorted non-PR dregs, drunks & junkies, various West 8th Streetwalkers of divers races, genders, ages. Bedbugs in my mattress. Endless gay insolence at the desk. A detailed dive.

Nevertheless, I stayed there from mid-August almost to the end of September. With all its disadvantages & squalor, the Winston was just too convenient to the 8th Street & Washington Square reservoirs of young flesh to be abandoned merely because of bedbugs. My dedication would be noble, had it any less outrageous an object. Here follow a few dirty stories from the Winston:

One: A 19-year-old, red-headed, baseball-playing, dope-peddling male prostitute encountered one 3 a.m. at the southwest corner of the Square. We went to my room & turned on, and then for $5 he let me blow him. This transpired thus: after consuming much grass, the lad more or less fell out sprawled across my bed. Tentatively, I touched him, moved my hand lightly to his crotch, farther, rubbed his penis toward erection. When it was hard & responding, pulse for pulse, to the pressure of my fingers, I made to undo his trousers. He said, in half a low whisper, "I hope you're willing to pay for it." This stunned me—it always does—but I managed to say,

"How much?" without losing my cool. "Five bucks," says he. This I can afford & I say so. Then he gets off the bed, strips, and returns to the bed, blank-faced. I join him & set to. It takes a good while, during which he sheds his impassivity & moans, grimaces, quakes & vigorously fucks. He comes long & convulsively, and then lies still, panting, in a near-swoon. I feel I've had my money's worth. Good sign.

Two: Eli, a 27-year-old Amerind just in from New Mexico, accosts me, 10 p.m., at the corner of West 8th & MacDougal, he sitting on the fireplug across from the bookstore, asking if I have someplace he can crash. I'm not expecting this & it startles me, puts me off. I shrug ruefully & continue on to the bookstore.

When I come out, he's still there, perched on the fireplug across the street. Hmmm. I peruse him. Aesthetically, he qualifies: somewhat shorter than I, trimly & athletically built, smooth skin soft-looking olive-gold, black hair, roundish Amerind-appealing face that looks younger than it could be. Sure.

So I ups to him & I says, "Still looking for a place to crash?" He is. I offer my room & off we go. He establishes himself, takes a shower, goes to bed. All kindness & benevolence, all virtue, I split, leaving him to sleep in peace. (What prompted this odd strategem I don't know.)

Return a few hours later, let my (quietly) self in without disturbing Eli, disrobe in darkness & crawl into bed. The mattress sags under the additional weight & Eli automatically compensates by sliding over closer to the wall, giving me more room. (It's a double bed.) This might mean he's awake, or it might not. Who can say?

We lie there, I faking stupor, a longish while, and then my left hand—plainly by accident & without conscious purpose—

brushes against his thigh—just, asleep, adjusting my arms to a more comfortable position—and lingers there. No response, either positive or negative, from Eli. This is to be expected, for Eli is theatrically asleep, lightly snoring, and this first contact is too tenuous to arouse him.

The idea is to establish contact without his noticing, so that later & more determined handwork will have had no perceptible beginning but seem to be continuation of something pre-existing his awareness and, therefore, presupposing his consent—not an attack but a constant, like the weight of the sheet. In theory, he's supposed thus to pass from sleep gradually to active participation without ever coming to wonder whether he really does consent or not, with consent assumed to have been given earlier: to glide from sleep to sex without thinking about it. Same old thing. Consensual rape is the name of the game, and I still don't know if it really works or not.

However, I get no more than halfway into this procedure— my hand cupped over the curve of his thigh, delighting slowly in the arc of that curve, my little finger braced against the edge of his briefs—halfway along, when Eli stirs, pauses, turns toward me, and puts his arm around my shoulder. Bingo.

We lie together, mouth to mouth, doubletonguing, while I cover all of him, span by span, with my slow-moving hands, rubbing every inch of him in reach with my fingertips, palm, whole hand flat, lightly, heavily, gently, now quivering, now serene, in every way I can, taking note of all his textures, the calculi of all his curves and hollows, of the soft deep skin over laborer's muscles, of the boundaries of hair, of the folds of his ears, of his buttocks—firm, beginning to stir—sliding smooth under the tight cotton of his briefs, grasping the graceful strength of his corded hips, the compound urgent barrels of his thighs—both hands poring over him sometimes symmetrically, sometimes contrapuntally—all through my incredible, greedy, conquering ritual of hands down to, at last, after teasing feints, cat-playing, down to his frantic cock, very hard but not long, vibrating—brush it, stroke it, rub it, handle it thoroughly in its cotton sheath & then slide down his belly & under his briefs like sneaking into a circustent to grasp it, flesh in flesh, fevered, and hold firm. I am a hand freak.

So off with the briefs & we belly-fuck joyfully. Then Eli, on top, sits back & spreads my legs. This I hadn't expected either. Eli is clearly proposing to bugger me. It's been six or seven years now since I was last fucked in the ass, and I'm a little apprehensive. Anal intercourse has been known to hurt. I really don't like pain.

But I'm not going to let the mere threat of pain interfere with a beautiful relationship. I know from experience that the worst it's likely to hurt is still bearable, and that it won't hurt any longer than Eli takes to penetrate & get established, which is very largely up to me. So I grab my knees & pull them down to my shoulders, elevating my asshole, and conscientiously relax.

Eli brings his head down, as if to blow me, and starts tonguing my asshole.

Shock! Also disgust. I try to maintain a clean asshole, and I'm freshly bathed, but a lot of shit has passed through that sphincter, and here is Eli running his tongue clockwise around it, pushing his firmwet tongue deep into it. I vividly imagine the taste of shit on his tongue (though I've never tasted shit myself) and nearly vomit. (In my early days as a fellator, the connection between piss & penis used to make me gag.)

But this is just a head trip. My body, which is now wholly centered on my asshole, is perfectly delighted with what's happening. ("Rimming," I later learn it's called.) This has never before been done to me, and it feels marvelous. Head quickly takes note of what body is saying, realizes Eli is doing what he wants to do, and abandons its imaginative prejudices. All discomfort is instantly gone, replaced by strong waves of (call it) warmth radiating from my asshole to every part of my body. I develop a new respect & fondness for my anus.

Eli keeps this up for some time, and I find myself—ordinarily a silent baller—moaning & squirming in unprecedented ecstasy. Then he slides his tongue slowly up (where does he get all this saliva?) over my balls, up the hysterical shaft of my cock, slowly, up my newly hyper-erogenous belly, up my chest, upward. Meanwhile his right hand guides his cock unerringly to my incandescent asshole, which welcomes him. A pause there, then a gentle shove, and his cock slides all the way into my ass while his body settles lightly down on mine and his right arm flows upward to join his left and hug me more than close. Another pause.

"Am I hurting you?" he whispers.

"Jesus, no!"

"Tell me if I hurt you," he says. "I don't want to hurt you," earnest, warm, sincere.

"It feels wonderful," I tell him.

And it does. Of course, it always feels good, once any initial awkwardness is overcome, to have a stiff cock up your ass. Back in 1955, in Hialeah, I was brutally ass-fucked by a stud who hoped thus (he claimed) to persuade me to give up my deviant ways, and it was great. But it's never felt as good as it does now, with Eli all but motionless (cock pulsing but not thrusting) within me.

"You're sure, now."

"Yes. Yes. Oh yes."

And slowly he begins to fuck.

Now, the usual ass fucking, in my experience, is a pretty perfunctory & even impersonal affair, as such things go. The fucker is generally an opportunist getting his rocks off in a convenient hole. His technique is sloppy: especially, his cock keeps falling out on the upstroke & having to be reinserted, which breaks up the rhythm & makes impossible any sort of elaborate, cumulative, sustained or otherwise sophisticated production. He gives no attention to detail: just ram, bam, thank you Sam. That the convenient hole he's fucking is my hole does not generally concern him. In fact, he's not fucking me, he's not even fucking, he's just jerking off in my ass. That I'm getting any pleasure out of his push-ups is purely coincidental. I suspect this is the standard American fucking style, wherefore American women so infrequently come. (That dude in Hialeah was a laudable exception. He really fucked, and he fucked really well, and I envy all his women.)

This kind of fucking is what I get, I guess, for being so absurdly hung up on straight puppies.

Eli, on the other hand, is a master, an artist, a glorious fuck. No one, no matter what his initial prejudices, could be fucked by Eli & regret it. The greatest possible *mutual* pleasure is Eli's goal, and he devotes his whole mind, his whole imagination, his whole body and an astonishing technical virtuosity to attaining it.

For instance, he is so pivoted on his knees that with every thrust the lower part of his body rises slightly, causing his cock to rub against my prostate gland in a manner calculated to reduce me to screaming & ecstasy. This same knee action rubs his soft belly & my cock together (it's very hot tonight

& we're both sweatslick & slippery), producing the closest approximation to a cunt I've experienced since the long-gone last ass *I've* happened to fuck—a closer approximation than that was, really.

Further, while doing this he also rotates slightly on his cock-axis, bringing joyful pressure to bear successively on every area of my rectum, giving great pleasure to nerve endings that haven't had anything interesting happen to them since I gave up being constipated, back in the 5th grade. This same rotation, of course, is likewise imparted via his belly to my cock.

Further, Eli's penis has its own consciousness. It never slips out of my ass, no matter how carried away we get, though he draws it daringly far enough out that my sphincter muscles are actively engaged. And he varies the speed & depth of his strokes in an acute & subtle way I still don't understand that keeps boosting the intensity of the experience beyond anything I've believed possible.

And all of this combined with an uncanny 'feedback circuitry' (perhaps some form of ESP) that keeps us moving together, in unison, throughout the fuck, with none of the discords of motion I've come to take for granted, till now, in even the best lays.

He's much better than I am, much better than anyone. Aside from following him perfectly through all this complex choreography, my only out of the ordinary contribution to it all is to exercise the control I've suddenly discovered I have over the muscles of my ass, 'milking' his cock as best I can.

Eli murmurs something complimentary, and fucks the more.

And thus we carry on at full symphonic length. Eli is inexhaustible, and I—though my back'll hurt tomorrow—am aware of nothing but the tropical pleasure Eli's administering to every part of me. Suddenly I understand all the *True Confessions/Modern Romances* stories I used to laugh at.

Eli can *fuck*!

And finally, after many false alarms & artful rushes, we come.

It gives me a hard-on just to write about it.

"Where did you learn to do that?" I ask him when I can.

"Inside," he tells me.

"Inside?"

"In the joint. You know, man. In jail."

"Is that what you do in jail?"

"You have to do something."

"What were you in jail for?"

"You know, man. They say I killed somebody."

I wonder how.

THREE

1970-1967

8/25/70 — L.A.

Repeated experience lately of listening to others making love has done me in. I'm OD'd on last straws. Sudden acute disintegration has rushed in. My mind is no longer my own, nor are my emotions, my reactions, even my words. I am exercising iron control now in all directions, to the very limits of my power. Within me rage, despair, anxiety, depression, anguish, bitterness, frustration, hate, all roil at top pressure. I can contain no more, can exert no more control.

My situation:

I sleep on a mat 3' by 5½' by 1½" thick upon the unclean floor of a narrow 'workroom' that will always smell of catpiss. Can't read in bed because the only light's a floodlight on the ceiling. Can't escape in sleep because the sun bursts through the uncurtained window onto my face at 0830, raising room temperature to 100+ for the next 12 hours.

I'm living out of suitcases. My papers are scattered, crumpled, torn, some destroyed or lost, all just barely accessible. My magical gear likewise, and likewise my books. To keep these safe from cats & kids, I have to keep everything in the workroom, where there is no room for anything.

Can't write because there is only the one small desk, which is Amy's, and because she objects to the kind of clutter I make working (I live here on sufferance), and because I've no place to keep notes & sketches conveniently to hand or to store scripts safe from childish harm, and because there's only the one typewriter, which is mine but which Amy uses sporadically to type the chart analyses whereby she supports herself & children (and also me), and because the children won't allow it by day, nor will Amy's social & sex life permit it by night, for the desk is in the bed-&-livingroom.

I have only as much privacy as is possible under the circumstances—a little more than none. Were I somehow to meet a candidate for sex, nothing c'd be done, for already Amy disapproves of my having visitors, and my sleeping quarters are too narrow for two people and too public for anything interesting.

My agent is dragging his heels on the book I miraculously wrote in June. In his latest letter he informs me there is no way to establish that *Probability Park* was ever submitted to Warner Bros/7 Arts and in passing that aside from desultory mail submissions no effort to sell *PP* to the movies was ever made.

This, at the same high level all the while, has been my situation for three months now, during which I have had no money, no peace, no hope, no sex, no anything.

And now I am well done in by it all.

My spirit is darkened. I catch myself thinking about death a lot, and though I squelch this every time I catch it, I still catch myself thinking about death a lot. Part of me is sure I'm going to die this year.

I've ceased to be charming and/or ebullient. My humor has grown mordant. My average mood is sad, morose. I am wholly without confidence, in self or anything. I've lost my charisma. I've ceased to assert myself. I've actually become self-effacing. I've developed the habit of subservience.

Mainly because I *am* here on love & sufferance, and wish to cause Amy the least possible inconvenience & disturbance.

I want to yell or scream or cry or rage. Instead I suppress almost all urges to self-expression, even the relatively harmless ones, for fear that if I let one thing out the lot will come tumbling after.

To keep our cramped conditions as pleasant as may be, I've managed, barely, to keep all this to myself and to preserve a generally calm & equable demeanor. This gets harder to do all the time.

I'm in a trap. Can't see any way out. My only hope—Jack Greeley at Esalen—is so tenuous, so baseless, even *I'm* not fooled by it.

I've no hope for the witchcraft book. It's doubtless sitting in Sandleman's files right now. Nor for *High Tea*, which Sandleman declines to resubmit because the fact that it's under contract to Grove may be a good selling point for film or foreign sale, though he declines to try for a film sale until the book is published.

I've suffered an extended & accelerating series of defeats, and I'm really beginning to feel defeated. What do you do in a case like that?

Shortly after the above, Ted Sarnoff offered to give me $60 a month toward rent on a place of my own, which sh'd in itself correct most of the conditions comprising my present misery.

From this, the Big Sur trip and similar positive elements lately seen, I permit myself the luxury of hoping maybe the curve has hit bottom & now is turning up again.

8/28/70 — L.A.

"I'm generally engaged in seducing whomever I'm with, but that's not what it seems. That's just how I learned to relate. And besides, I hardly ever score."

"How come?"

"I'll do anything but ask."

"Oh. You want it to be *their* idea."

"It seldom is."

8/29/70 — L.A.

All that kept me unlaid last night was my stupid prejudice against faggots. A pretty boy is a pretty boy, straight or gay regardless. And this one last night, who was on the blond brink of my door before he spoke & gave himself away, this one was a very pretty boy, and sufficiently butch if he'd kept his mouth shut.

Why do I so recoil from the gay? Even sweet Andrew put me in trauma when he went down on me in New York—Steven Arnold's bed, another bug ranch.

Don't know. My objection to the screaming swishes is reasonable enough: I yam what I yam, and if I ever *want* a woman, I have real ones available. But to extend this to last night's blond boy is absurd, and I don't know why I do it.

(Hypothesis: fear of proving inadequate in a fully recipro-cal situation with an experienced partner? Fear of methedrine impotence? Perverse obsession with the relative innocence of a crashed boyman with my unexpected hand in his crotch? Delight in violating the unwary? Mix 'em or match 'em.)

I'd probably score higher with less speed. Speed keeps me walking, and walking fast. Last night I was the fastest thing on the sidewalk. Covered the whole turf bounded by Argyle, Sunset, Whittel & Hywd five or six times, with breaks at my room betweentimes to scribble.

Whereas, if I had stayed in one place, loitering, or drifted very slowly, I'm sure I'd've scored handily. This cross-country style's been too long upon me—even before speed. Tonight—remind me—I'll try & do the other thing.

What I did to my father has happened to me some 10,000 times so far & I'm beginning to understand the old man.

What's the use of being sexually liberated if nobody else is?

"What's your favorite restaurant?"
"Levi's."

I am not the kind of person I w'd ever go to bed with, and I can't understand why the people who *do* go to bed with me do so.

I have an abnormally dirty mind. It has been my fortune, for it operates typewriters. Otherwise, I always have to make allowances for it. To wit: nobody means by any smile or gesture what my mind believes is meant. This is more inconvenient than sad, for when they *do* mean it I can't tell.

Met tonight at Amy Kidd's a boy named Blake about whom it is hard to write without falling into gush. He's a Leo, 17+, blond, blue-eyed, vital, 5'11", slender, bright & beautiful, a veteran of debauchery & radiant with joy. Oh my.

Blake's a glorious example of the new man we've been, sporadically consciously, working to create. As such, he's nearly as alien to us as he is to his Bircher parents, for we've had no way before to determine the effect of removing the hangups we've sought mainly out of faith to cure, only that the effects of the hangups themselves being clearly bad, the effect of removing them ought hopefully to be good. And we ourselves are only as imperfectly free of these hangups as we've been able by acts of will to make ourselves, a far cry from the freedom of never having had them.

So. Blake's ways are not quite ours, though we can appreciate them. His standards are maybe just within our ability to imagine, but probably not. In him we can unsurely recognize structures of value & taste, of liberty & brotherhood, all made real & functioning, that we know only as ideals. Thus his morality is as free & sympathetic as we've hoped it would be, and much freer than we can make our own. He's both our product and, in a sense, our superior, or enough so to be not entirely comprehensible—or, maybe, not entirely credible. I think we never really expected to succeed.

And for all of this, he's not a great deal freer of hangups than we, but his are different from our own. Doubtless he in turn, or in their turn his kids, will work toward an improvement of the race as we toward him. Man cannot become perfect, but is infinitely perfectible. Always improvements are possible, always the old gives way to the new, always new perfections breed new flaws. And it does this pious child molester's spirit good to see this Blake of beauty rising while I'm still young enough to appreciate him.

He's a universal head, willing to take any drug that offers pleasure, most unlikely to get hooked. He likes to drink, too; to get drunk. During the evening he consumed half a pint of bourbon, at least two pints of beer & a wealth of hash, with no ill effect. In fact, when I arrived & encountered him at four he was glowing—really—and sober, and when I left at eleven he was still apparently sober but glowing much more brightly.

He's a guitar player—a good one, Amy says—and intends to go to college to study theory &c, to become a musician. His idea of what there is for him to learn about music is rudimentary, but it's clear that the deeper he gets into it, the deeper he'll want to go. This is suggested by the excitement with which he listened to me rap, on speed as usual, about the joys of music, the endless chain of new & groovy things to know. When *I* was 17—when I was at the U of M, for that matter—my peers were dismayed by the wealth of knowledge music offered. Blake's delighted. So was I.

He's so nearly (not quite) liberated sexually we, at his age, had no words to describe his condition. He's evidently straight enough: he digs girls; but he doesn't seem particularly averse to any brand of sex. He's slept with men as well as women, and done everything within the homo repertoire, but it seems to bother him that he enjoys girls more. Ours being a compact society, Blake's several times played trios with Emil Bach & Judy Milan.

(Notice in passing that there doesn't seem to be anything

it bothers Blake to tell about himself. At his age I couldn't've told a priest the half of what he's fairly unimpressed by. In fact, I originally left the Church, back in 1949 in Jacksonville, to avoid having to tell a priest about my mutual masturbation games with Ed Bronson, or my nightly games of solitaire.)

Blake's drawn to older, more experienced, maybe wiser people, gurus of a sort. This is why he was visiting Amy. He instantly establishes an Athenian relationship with every sage, however specialized, he meets: the absolute, ultimate flattery. Blake's rabid for enlightenment. What kind of an adult will he become?

He's Amy's regular baby sitter, though I don't really know why he was there this afternoon. (I presume friendship.) Writing this, suddenly my mind starts conning plots to get Amy out of the house & he in it on schedule for a useful length of time.

I came in & saw him glowing on the couch & was amazed. Also tentatively despairing, for I'd seen many glorious puppies in Amy's old East 6th Street pad who might better have been in Dubuque for all the access I had to them. The moment I saw him I knew that in 15 minutes he'd have to go home & the accident that introduced us would never happen again, or that he was only passing through L.A. en route to somewhere else, or however how unreachable, and I despaired.

Somewhat later he asked me if I'd take a long uphill walk with him to buy him a bottle of bourbon, but I was wearing new shoes & my feet hurt. In the course of discussing his drinking habits, I being opposed from reflex, he mentioned that booze stimulated him to rap. It having by then been arranged that Amy would eventually drive over & buy him his bourbon, I promptly (expecting nothing) invited him to stay & do his drinking & rapping with us, on the ground,

created therewith, that I wanted to get the younger generation's reactions to & thoughts about *Pigs & Fishes*. (To plan
the magazine was the official reason I was there.)

So it came to pass. We three—Blake, Amy & I—rapped, all
on hash & he on bourbon as well, at first about the magazine,
then about the thinking behind it, and then for hours on phi-
losophy, morality, ethics, sex & metaphysics, all as related to
Blake & his experience. I was wired on 125 mgs of Dexedrine
plus all that hash, and I'd been studying the Ching intensely
of late & holding long spiritual discussions with Melinda
Black, as well as with Amy, and thus spoke with incredible
wisdom & clarity, wit & style—the best possible way to talk
to Blake.

And tomorrow we're to do it again with a tape recorder
catching it, and rap a lovely article for *Pigs & Fishes*. Count
on it, I'll devise a way to incorporate Blake into the *P&F*
staff before the evening ends.

Consider how Blake's affair with Emil & Judy started. He
& Emil went to Emil's pad. There Emil gave him two dime
bags of methedrine to sniff—a monster dose even for me.
Then they blew grass. (Emil always has the finest dope in
town.) When Blake was properly high—and that combination
of drugs leads to instant enlightened confusion—Emil adroitly
assaulted him, gave him an erection before he fully knew
what was happening, and they were off. A little later Judy
came home & the sport diversified. Even though he didn't
properly enjoy Emil—by which he means that he enjoyed
Judy more—Blake went back for additional helpings we never
did establish just how many times.

It's quite understandable that Emil, or any person of
taste, would fairly or foully have at Blake the first chance he
got, raping him with speed. (Not the drug I'd've chosen. Acid

w'd be far better. But maybe speed's all Emil had on hand.) I hope to do much the same sort of thing with Blake myself. Nothing else would make sense.

Blake inspires instant tender Blakelust in everyone he meets—I saw this happen when visitors passed through—and no one who can sense this can resist it. All of his beauties are meant to be touched, and he likes to be touched. He is awesomely desirable & radiates desire. I have no way to describe any of this adequately to anyone who can't experience it. The melting beauty of a boy is hard for a really heterosexual man to perceive or admit: it's so much more than visual, but eyes are all a straight man dares to use. Lines, curves, handscapes of flesh more exquisite than any female body shows, more graceful & alive, the strength of his beauty—and more than a body for mine to glorify, but a mind of equal beauty wanting always to be taught, to be to my mind what his body is to mine ... To fuck a boy's just high-class jerking off; to make love to a boy you have to teach him something.

All of which is still just fantasy. Our physical intimacy so far is limited to my resting my arm on his leg once whilst lighting the toke pipe for him while Amy & the kids were out doing the laundry. This tiny contact gave him an erection, though. There are no secrets between us.

But now I'm caught. All of a sudden I'm motivated. Obsessed. I'm trapped in Los Angeles at least until we've slept together, more likely, if we do, until we quit. If we do. Blake has become my primary project, toward which all my other schemes are now stepping stones, and thus certain of accomplishment.

The object is to get him alone—it may be all right for Emil, but I don't want to share Blake with a woman—fill him up with the proper fuel—acid, of course, if there's any real acid available, or maybe we can throw a drunk together—and worship the Tao in him with every sense I own.

Getting him alone might be a problem. There's little hope of privacy at Amy's, he lives with his parents, and unless he has access to a car I haven't heard about, my room's impractically far away. Still, I *might* be able to get him to my room—if he doesn't mind an eight block walk, the public transportation's almost adequate—but I'll have to plant an inducement here sufficiently attractive to justify his making the trip. Perhaps a quart of bourbon will suffice. I'll see.

Of course, I could just invite him over for sex, but that w'd be most unlike me, and w'd give him the opportunity to decline. Keep the matter open till the matter opens us. If I don't bring sex up, Blake can't put it down. So much for honesty.

(The hexagram I threw for Blake is 35, Progress. The powerful prince is honored with horses in large numbers. In a single day he is granted audience three times. If the oracle is speaking of Blake in terms of my desires—and there's no reason why she shouldn't be, for they occupied most of my mind while I was throwing the coins, as they do now—this is a groovy oracle, full of double entendre (audience three times in a single day) & promise.)

5/10/68

In last night toward the end of the *I Ching* class at Amy's came the unflawed Blake—beerdrunk to wobbling, roaringly eager to complicate matters with hash—who proceeded to inundate me with improper advances.

Since this was plainly impossible, I assumed that once again my drug-stained mind was reading implications &

suggestions into his speech & behavior that he neither intended nor was aware of—my perceptions warped by my desires. Accordingly I took care not to respond to the erotic suggestions I imagined I was imagining.

The 'illusion' intensified as my outward response continued to be nonerotic & proper. It was a convincing illusion, but I've been there, so I told myself, "This isn't really happening," and blamed it on the hash, saying, "Wow! *Good* hash!" when Blake rested his hand by chance upon my knee.

A little later I drew Amy aside to compare notes. She also had the impression that Blake was proliferating passes at me. I was glad it wasn't the hash; Blake is prettier.

Blake's advances: sitting crosslegged on the floor beside me, smoking hash, he promoted pseudo-chance physical contact—his hand brushing my leg & lingering; our fingers touching/trembling during the hashpipe ceremony, and later in same resting his forehead against my wrist as he toked, then running his free fingers over my face as I toked, all officially accidental, all under pretense of pipe lighting; staring at me, liplicking smile, long at a time.

He also talked at length about Emil Bach, praising him with great praise, expressing profoundest love/admiration for him. Blake lived with Emil & Judy recently. He spoke vaguely but fondly of this period, emphasizing the erotic aspects of his relationship with Emil with progressively increasing energy & candor.

Segue to his worries about the draft, a problem still fairly remote from him. (How did I feel about the draft at 17? I don't recall thinking much about it until I was 18 & in college. Even then it didn't much excite me, though I enlisted in the Navy partially to escape the draft. Perhaps knowing the Navy was waiting for me spared me the draft hangup.)

Blake acted out for us his plan to fag out of the draft—trying unsuccessfully to imitate stereotyped fag limp wrist & effete speech. He repeated this performance several times, augmenting it each time with additional data & detail. Hilarity increased to match.

You couldn't tell whether his claim to be homosexual was a fiction for the Army or, masquerading as such fiction, a statement of what he thinks to be fact, aimed at my ears. He bases his claim on having lived intimately with a homosexual for a month. (Meaning Emil. But Emil's not gay. Blake doesn't understand his own strange power: in his presence few men can help being/becoming queer for him, I think, but that doesn't make them gay. Given the opportunity, not balling Blake's more unnatural than blowing a regiment.) Thinks maybe he should live in such sin with yet another homosexual for a while, just to be on the safe side. Allows as how he likes living with homosexuals. (I'm impressed.)

Dissolve to a general discussion of the gay life. Of being cruised & solicited from passing cars on Hywd Blvd. Of getting hastily blown in the front seats of such cars. Comments on the eyes of homosexuals, the way they look at him & at each other & the world. Touches on the various kinds of homosexual, how they live & act, what they do, taking care to point out that some homosexuals are perfectly straight in everything else. (I was too wasted to recognize this as a fishing expedition, an invitation to declare myself. Hmm.) Claims to dig it all. (Interesting.)

The subject of booze ariseth. I mention the fifth of Cutty Sark in my dresser drawer. He says he's not tried Scotch—he's only 17, after all—and would like to see what it does to him. I invite. Blake accepts.

Although it was already 0100, late, Blake decided that much rather than go home, he wanted to come to my pad with me right now & experience Scotch &c &c. However, Marc, my ride, although avowedly very tired, spent 20 minutes saying goodnight, and by the time we were ready to leave, Blake had changed his mind (probably, considering his parents, wisely).

He postponed it until tonight. "It's Friday," he explained, "so I'll be able to spend the night with you." Yay!

Then Blake walked home, half a block, and Marc & I drove off into the void.

This journal depicts me as obsessively preoccupied with sex. The impression is not quite accurate. It's a sporadic obsession only—but then, this is a sporadic journal, and I've come to it lately mainly to record triumphs or protracted bouts of failure.

Part of the present situation is that I've been ruined by Allen. Sex isn't what I am after, sex is what I can get. What I want is another matter. If Blake were to decide to live with me for a month, that might be a month of it.

It (all the 'it's in the two paragraphs above) has somewhat to do with reconstructing my self-confidence, destroyed last May/June when the communication company fell and only now beginning to re-form. I'm not at all sure how they are related, only that they are & that 'success' in the one is therapeutic for the other.

So. I don't really expect Blake to appear tonight, though I'll put no obstacles in his way & make such preparations for his visit as I can. Blake is 17 and has had lots of time since 0130 to change his mind or to forget. It furthers one to remember that he's still a boy, not wisely to be depended on.

If indeed he doesn't show, I'll be more than disappointed, but he's already done more for me last night than most of the host I've slept with ever did.

To have been pursued & wooed with such determination & vigor by so consummately beautiful a boy—far & gone the loveliest male since that September '65 accidental pickup at Grand Central Station, and of his age (in itself a transcendent beauty) the finest since my MacDougal Street puppyromp of 1960-62, prior to which my memory tends to clothe every bedmate in unreal beauty—to have been, to however small avail, the object of such attention from such a boy has in itself (subjectively appraised) done more to restore my confidence than any other event in eleven months.

Anyhow, I don't expect him to arrive, but if he happens to, I mean to be as dissolute, decadent & all-embracing as it is in me to be, and ball as though sex were due to be repealed come noon tomorrow. Blakes are rare in both my life & the real world. That Blake will spend the night with me even once is unlikely enough that if it happens it must be made the most of. And if he makes a habit of visiting me, each time must likewise be grokked in its fullness & cherished. There is no tomorrow. Never has been, but at 35—especially if you're a puppy lover—your awareness of no tomorrow is acute, and Allen taught me the importance of perseverance in bed.

Query: how many more 17-year-old beauties am I likely to be blessed with? Right.

(And I stand ready to do whatever I can to help Blake beat the draft.)

Meanwhile, what am I to make of last night? What turned Blake on to me so drastically? My previous encounters with him did nothing to prepare me for such unbridled affection.

I don't know anything much about the boy, really, not even his last name. (Oh, that he was busted for dealing & released in his parents' custody, but that's no help.) Amy, of course, has told me all about him, but she spoke entirely in astrologese & left me uninformed. Disregarding aesthetics, I know this:

> digs sex
> digs dope
> digs booze
> digs older men
> good guitarist
> wants to learn theory &c
> intelligent, but not a reader
> made it with Emil for a month
> has had other homosexual experience

With this for a dossier, who can make predictions? However, when I realized last night that it wasn't the hash, I threw a change on Blake (as he was then, including all potential relationships) & got 11, Peace to 57, The Gentle. "When ribbon grass is pulled up, the sod comes with it. Each according to his kind. Undertakings bring good fortune." Also, "The sovereign I gives his daughter in marriage. This brings blessing & supreme good fortune," both of which sound better than good. Plus the sixth line, as usual, screaming Too much. Too far. Hold back. But then 57.

This all sounds favorable enough, but what it has to do with tonight is still unknown.

10:30 p.m. & still no trace of Blake. Where is the ribbon grass? Where the king's daughter? If he's not here by 12 or so, I'll amble over to Libbi & Jim's & scrounge a meal perhaps.

Questions arise.

Have I been stood up, or is he planning to come here after some more orthodox date? If he's changed his mind, why hasn't he phoned? Was he so stoned last night that he doesn't remember anything of it? Has he been distracted & let it slip his mind? Has he . . . fuck it.

(Perhaps I am beginning to learn about Blake.)

Blakeless midnight. What a drag. Not a serious drag, nor yet an unfamiliar one, but still, there are times when I hate being right.

5/12/68

Blake couldn't make it last night because of parent problems. Dealing with the young has disadvantages.

This being the day of the full moon in Scorpio, a day of great occult import, Amy had some of her wizard friends over to celebrate &c. Included were Kenny, an astrologer/ Subudite, Don Walters & myself. Blake also showed up. Real invitations need never be mailed.

Blake & I went out & bought a six-pack of Colt-45. Thereafter throughout the evening we drank thereof & necked outrageously. Don finally took Amy to Kaleidoscope. Blake & I thereupon necked even more outrageously, despite Kenny's lingering. (He obviously wanted to play.)

Finally Ken left & we grew yet more outrageous. High order necking & kissing, the sort of activity Father Francis Xavier used to warn us kids against, but not exactly sex. We kept our clothes on, for example, but our hands were under them. Blake claims only women rouse him. We'll test that later.

Eventually (0200) Terragoo & Billy LeMont entered, cooling things. Blake planned to come home with me, but finally split to his pad for a hamburger instead.

I'm beginning to feel not unlike Humbert Humbert.

5/15/68

Blake finally made it to my pad, and we consumed an awful lot of Scotch. The level of erotic intensity was extremely high, though not a drop of semen did we shed. Blake feared he had hemorrhoids, and nothing would do but for him to drop his pants and have me examine his asshole. Then, since the absence of trousers made clothes per se ridiculous, we both stripped & examined each other in great detail, visually & manually, while swilling down whiskey like milk. I did my best to teach Blake to see his own beauty—never, I suspect, a difficult task when the student's 17—and probably succeeded. He tried to teach me my beauty, with less success but no less pleasure.

When we couldn't stand up anymore we lay down & slept together, naked, in each other's arms. No sex—we were both too drunk for erections—but it didn't seem necessary. Joy is a naked boy, the ancients said.

(1977: For several months we were together frequently, but none of that entered my journal, where I wrote of desire & triumph, but never of long fulfillment. "But of bliss and glad life there is little to be said, before it ends; as works fair and wonderful, while still they endure for eyes to see, are their own record, and only when they are in peril or broken

forever do they pass into song." And then, in June, I left Los
Angeles. But:)

12/4/70 — L.A.

Last week Blake showed up after two years' absence. I woke
around 1300 & staggered into the livingroom, and there he
was, rapping with Amy. What a nice way to wake up.

All the aesthetic commentary on him still applies, except
he's almost 20 now, and is hereby incorporated herein by
reference.

Seems Blake's been these two years in the Coast Guard &
is not at all happy about it. He's home on leave from Oregon
& has decided not to go back. (All during the long discussion
of this we flirted very tentatively.) I outlined the drawbacks
of desertion, Amelia seconding.

Instead, I said, go to your base psychiatrist & give him a
full & graphic history of your sex life. Your games two years
ago with Emil & with me are sufficient grounds for a General
Discharge—Under Honorable Conditions, which is hardly
painful at all & is better than doing time in a Naval prison.

He saw the sense of this, and elaborated that his sex life
has become more complicated these two years. Even though
Coast Guard duty runs to long periods—months—with not a
woman in sight, Blake has not been sexually deprived. He &
his fellow Guards have—perforce, he claims, still not knowing
his own power—served each other well.

(Blake is still wholly unhesitant about saying anything at
all, but especially things I'd work up an ulcer trying to figure
out how to express.)

Amy & I assured him that this was his ticket to ride. He

was persuaded, convinced, agreed with us & decided to do it so. One wonders what he'll do.

Whereupon, unwarned of, Amy grabbed Jennifer & split for somewhere, leaving us together. Oh.

We look, talk, smile a short time—he sitting on the bed, I on a chair. I get up, join him on the bed, and without signals pull him over & into a clinch. He says, "You're a horny old man." I like it.

Blake says, "This isn't right. Let's take our clothes off." Right on.

We get off the bed & strip. I lock the never-locked front door. We clinch & grope & grind standing, then topple onto the bed. Yay.

Blake's body is such a joy to traverse.

We play hot tete a tete a while (never long enough), all possible matching parts & organs in all possible contact—the old interfemoral routine—sans penetration. Blake doesn't have an erection—"Somehow I can only get a hardon with a chick"—but that doesn't matter. He doesn't seem to miss it, he's having a good time, and—on this occasion—I've got enough for the two of us.

During this I get an insight into Blake's sexuality. He digs the yin role. Passive in an energetic way. Digs being fucked by strangers, or older, or more aggressive, or wiser—whatever— men. By them. He doesn't want to fuck them, he wants to be fucked.

(The liberated Blake I saw in '68 was not the Blake that was/is, but the Blake that is/was was/is good enough. Someone else's hangups often seem like none at all, if they're not your own. I imagine I'll learn . . .)

I'm willing to oblige. There's no cock that wouldn't like to move across the soft skin of Blake's belly, no rod that would not appreciate that friendly boyhand closing on it, no me who would not appreciate the intensity of Blake's cooperation.

Then he shows me what he learned in the Coast Guard. He learned how to give head. It comes as a shock—especially after the protracted negotiations & hangups of two years ago —to find myself suddenly up to the hilt in Blake's mouth. I have no complaint at all, but it's certainly not what I'd expected.

He's good. The Coast Guard taught him well. I can't remember when I've enjoyed a blow job more.

And now he's back in Oregon, fruiting himself out of the service. If the psychiatrist asks Blake for proof, Blake'll be back with us inside of a month.

(He explained the absence of a hardon thus, as he cast aside his g.i. shorts & approached, golden, for that first naked clinch: "It's girls who turn *me* on, but I like giving pleasure to people." Strange youth. A book or two lie hidden in young Blake.)

10/28/67 — L.A.

Unknown person of doubtful acceptability found occupying my bed at Ed & Barbara's when we got home from playing at the Ash Grove. Long & silent interfemoral fuck. Possibility he hath a pox—some sort of growth on penis. Came three times fully clothed, and when I woke up he was gone. I wonder who he is.

11/11/67

That unknown person turns out to be a cousin of Ed's, whose name I still don't know. When I encountered him, he'd left (somehow) some mental hospital somewhere in California six days before & spent the intervening time on the road. According to Barbara, his problem is that he isn't sure what his gender is or ought to be, and is chronically (a) depressed & (b) entering into ambiguous sexual situations therefor. No more do I know save that he's still at Ed's place, talks little, and is generally either drunk or drinking. He strikes me as a poor insurance risk.

He is, however, acceptably pretty, and hath not a pox. Glad tidings.

1/28/68

Clear & cold at 7 a.m. after a day of gray rain.

On 8th June last I suddenly, unexpectedly began to sleep

alone again after four warm months, and I'm still not used to
it. Any bed at all's too big for one. All my desire is to do it
again, and I don't know how.

I am hung up on love & inept at sex. I am unable to pick
up puppies who are all but saying out loud Let's do it. One
streetcorner boy last night, for instance, was making sexual
motions & gestures, pointing at his crotch with a twitching
middle finger, tapping his foot in codelike spaced rhythms,
looking very earnestly at me & licking slowly his lips . . . and
I refused to believe it. Fear of misunderstanding froze my
mind. What's wrong with me? If I can't take anyone to bed
to begin with, with whom can I hope to share bed & lifelines?

Yet I've had already this year two ballings, both one-
nighters I'd've gladly extended if I knew how. At 0300 January 1, portentous reball of Ed's mad cousin Willow (that's
his name), after intriguing psychodrama foreplay:

Willow (first time we're alone—we're crashing in the livingroom after a party—brusquely): I suppose you're expecting
to screw me again.

Valentine (shocked): Well . . .

Willow (almost apologetic): Well, forget it. I mean, too
much to drink . . . don't feel good . . .

(Silence.)

Much later, long after lights out, maybe a mostly silent
hour, I find myself too yearning to sleep (there's nothing
more conducive to insomnia for me than to have a puppy
sleeping solo in another bed in the same room with me; dormitory life w'd be pure hell), so I get up off my pallet on the
floor & stumble hushedly through the darkness toward the
overstuffed chair, where I intend to smoke pot until I can
sublimate my hunger, but:

Willow (still brusque): Why don't ya' get in bed with me?

Valentine (hypershocked): What?

Willow: C'mon. (rolling over) Get in bed with me.

Valentine sheds clothes & leaps in. Remembering Willow's confusions, I maneuver him from his initial female/passive role to a terminal male/active one, thinking 'twould be good for him. After the dust settled, he complained about this.

Aside from being a nut, Willow is aesthetically satisfactory—tall, skinny, hand-carved, taut, almost fragile—acceptably intelligent & cultivably talented in some obvious but unspecified way, maybe artistic. This w'd be an interesting, entertainingly horny pup to live with, but easy as it is to arrange to be invited into bed with this young man—*his* bed—I've no idea how to get him to live with me.

That is, I don't know what I can offer him, because (among other things) he doesn't talk much to anybody (not only me). We've had only the two brief conversations recorded here—about six lines each, and starkly explicit: basically, technical communications; he only talks to ask me into bed, which is nice as far as it goes but doesn't tell me much. So I know his extravagant sexual complexity in some detail, but I don't know what he likes that isn't sex.

My estimates of his intelligence, talent & compatibility are based solely on "vibes"—a non-specific, non-verbal, irrationally poetic subjective assessment, catastrophically fallible (but so far I've been lucky). Vibrations—but I don't know what to talk about. I don't know what role it is that *I'm* supposed to play.

With Larry Marcus, on the other hand, role is no problem. Larry is a 19-year-old political activist who comes as an occasional bonus for playing left-wing fun & games with Fred Heller. Since Fred & I live far apart in this transit desert of L.A., now & then Larry has been my chauffeur.

Larry is—how shall we say it—very *healthy*, in a healthy sort of way. A good American boy ("American" as a race), his family may well be from Ohio or Idaho—farm & milkfed health country. Unlike the East Coast, Los Angeles was settled principally from other parts of the same country—U.S. of A.— and the prevailing physical standards (see any mass magazine color photo story about California. Dig the hair, faces, bodies— these fair, solid, spirited young animals, all, even the homely, somehow goodlooking in all the same way, indefinably radiant (poverty an ancestral myth) grandchildren of those WPA post office murals, a trifle ubermenschlich—better fed, housed, clothed, educated, entertained, fucked & slaughtered in the mass than the heroes of antiquity (pre-World War 1½) individually—a nearly master race & prone to think so, quite politely) are not what we're accustomed to back east.

An order of physical beauty obtains here as the norm for the sub-middle class, for the masses—an unperceived background against which yet another order of beauty is determined—that no genetically filtered aristocracy approaches. Everyone on the East Coast, however awesomely beautiful, is lesser, more tense & unsure, less healthy, physically inferior to the West Coast norm. Madmen, even, while maddest in L.A., less in touch with reality, are yet amazingly survival-prone—maniacs who couldn't live ten years in Manhattan run for office in L.A. And win!

What that demented, speedy rhapsody was centered on is this:

L.A. puppies average prettier than most, and Larry's L.A. average, maybe better, which is good enough for me.

He's a peculiarly squarish kid trying too hard to be hip, given to hero worship, whose radical commitment's probably linked to some crisis of identity. Bright enough, but dogma-prone. A born disciple, a follower, a student.

> Roy smiled at me gently and said, "Well the way to hold on to a girl is to be cool. I'm indifferent to them, see, and they know it and keep after me. I ignore them and they come back for more . . . Do you want to know how to hold on to a girl or how to hold on to a boy?"
>
> "A boy," I allowed.
>
> "To hold a boy," he said softly, "you have to teach him something."

(Irving Rosenthal: Sheeper,
Grove Press, 1967)

Larry's a head shorter than I, which I appreciate, stocky but beautifully molded. He's built in rectangular solids: a small one slightly taller than broad for his head, a very broad one for his shoulders, a much narrower one for hips, all edges rounded & softened with a swimmer's musculature. Crewcut hair joblot brown; plain/attractive boyface, innocent verging on dumb; quick-smiling (nervous) perfect many teeth; blue eyes maybe scared; unwholesome craving for acceptance. His dad's an ultraconservative former Army officer who'd shoot the boy if he knew the company he keeps.

I met Larry at Fred's in November & desired him, but he was so vigorously straight I instantly rejected the possibility & relegated him to fantasy. Never came on to him, never considered it. Hands to myself. Rode weekly hours across the L.A. ruins with him in mild discomfort. Never even asked the oracle.

Until January 11th. Long politically heavy secret meeting at Freddie's with some Marxists to plan the American Youth

Festival in Chicago, which is to coincide with the Democrats'
national convention. Much ceremonial pot smoking to prove
that the Marxist is just one of the boys, myself containing
quite some speed. Youthful Folly, very dull.

On the way home, maddened by dope & dialectic & having cautiously established that Larry had nothing to do in the
morning, I nervously semi-invited him to spend the night
with me & he said Yes.

My confusion spoke fluent hysteria, panic suppressed like
a sneeze. I've never been able to cope with good fortune. This
can't mean what I want it to, but what else can it mean?

Crossing the mountains, I outlined the end of the world,
which I'm almost certain is at hand. Famine, plague, revolution, war, ruin—I was horribly eloquent, and Larry was
impressed.

Home at last, we blow more grass. Larry falls out on my
bed. (When we get right down to the action, my memory
reverts to present tense.) I sit disbelieving & polite upon the
couch, scared shitless. Larry sleeps. Time passes.

I collect the stash, douse the light, sit without rational
justification on the edge of the bed & smoke a lot of grass,
painstakingly evolving feather-tip contact with his knee, I
trembling at the edges with doubt. This goes on for a very
long time.

So he says, "Wow, man, what a hangup," pitying, which
hurts, and we ball with great enthusiasm & ingenuity thereafter, I still not completely free of doubt.

It turns out he's a virgin, altogether, and he thanks me for
correcting that defect. (It's hard for me to believe in a 19-
year-old male virgin, all my experience is against it, but I suppose that there are lots of them around.)

And my only problems now are that I haven't seen him

since—no travelling, not while Fred's playing with Marxists—
and that I don't understand a bit of it.

Otherwise, despite opportunities I've been unable to
bring myself to grasp, I've slept alone & not been glad of it.

(1977—Looking back on it, I realize I was caught throughout
that time in a textbook drug psychosis, and I wonder how I
managed to survive. They tell you Speed Kills but they never
tell you what. There's a lot of that psychosis in this book.)

FOUR

Jacksonville

My cherry was fin'ally excised by Edward T. Riley in 1947, the fall thereof, or maybe early 1948. The confusion of dates (it was probably spring '48) is because my family'd just been transferred from Dallas to Jacksonville, Florida, where all the seasons look alike. I was, anyhow, a sophomore at Robert E. Lee High School, a honcho in the band, and so was Eddie.

Fifteen I was, and ignorant. My virtue, which I'd been willing—eager—to shed since 1945, had been assailed again & again in Dallas, to—purely through my own Irish-Catholic ignorance—no avail. Naked male bodies, and especially naked male bodies in bed with me, had long since (1943) been an obsession of mine, but—being Irish-Catholic & having a very narrow view of the matter—I'd never equated this preoccupation with, dare I say it, sex. I was so ignorant that the following early erotic experiences didn't register as erotic at all:

In Dallas (all of this digression is in Dallas) Henry Adams & I used to go swimming bare-assed in a nearby gravel pit. (Amazing, the differences among bare-assed, naked & nude.) In the natural course of events we'd interact physically, wrestling et cetera. Penes'd erect, as they will. Henry, who, though my age, knew more than I, w'd make sexual allusions. I, being I, w'dn't recognize them. No matter. We'd go on rubbing against each other, getting our rocks off before we/I knew we had rocks at all.

Digression still. Joe Rockwell, a peer (now a dentist, of all things), trombonist in my jr. high school band (I was premier flautist therein), & I used to spend the night together

—a natural consequence of our age—frequently. We'd lie abed huddled together like nested teaspoons talking the most arrant nonsense about Sex (it was always uppercase then), our inevitable & recurrent genital contact never remarked upon. Each of us, it later turned out, was waiting for the other to make the first move. The first move was never made.

And (digression still) Lowell Sullivan, red-haired & freckled, another flute player, one grade ahead of me, whom now I'd ball without a moment's thought, used fairly often to spend the night with me, doing his 14-year-old best to seduce the idiot virgin I was, to no effect.

One of the last nights I spent in Dallas—the family'd already gone to Jacksonville, and I was just staying behind to finish a summer course in harmony at SMU—Lowell, Joe & I spent the night a trois at Lowell's house. With a casual handsweep Lowell evaluated the groins of Joe & myself & took Joe off to another room, leaving me to sleep alone & unaware of what was going on.

Four years later we, all three, made up for this absurdity, but that was four years later.

The only overtly sexual experience I had at that time (still digression) was with Tim Gibson, age 9. His father, a commander, had bought our Dallas house, having been transferred there from San Diego, and the Gibson family moved in after my family'd left but before I finished my summer course. They got established, sort of, then Cmdr & Mrs G went away, leaving me to babysit Tim.

Despite his youth, Tim'd had infinitely more sexual experience than I was going to have for several years. He'd been, in fact, the prime sex object of an L.A. puppy-cult, getting his tiny cock sucked several times a day in the restroom of a gas station on Santa Monica Boulevard. (My life, and probably yours, is full of these absurd resonances.) When his family went off for their vacation or whatever, Timmy insisted on sleeping with me. I had no objections.

Little Timmy introduced me to the art of mutual masturbation. In fact, little Timmy was the first person other than myself or my mother (a splendid digression going begging there) who ever touched my penis. I was quite grateful but, in the strictest possible sense, nothing ever came of it. Though he told me all about his L.A. experiences, I was not a bit tempted to suck him off (for one thing, people piss through those things, and I wasn't ready to get a mouthful of urine), and he explained that my cock, and his boyfriends in L.A.'s, was much too large for him to suck—a lie. Nevertheless we enjoyed a lot of manual stimulation.

When the adult Gibsons returned, Tim, for some reason, told them all about what we'd been up to. This led to the most amazingly low key denunciation I've ever been the victim of. They even sent a letter to my family in Jacksonville, of which I never heard a word.

No matter, no matter, no matter. Within a week I was on a Delta DC-3 en route to Jacksonville, en route to Eddie Riley & the whole real world.

Eddie Riley was tall & sunny, elegantly slim, with dark but glowing brown hair, luminous gentle brown eyes (almost bovine, but livelier), lightly tanned & finely molded face, brilliant white teeth, startling, that flashed at you hundreds of times an hour in his ready lightning stroke of a smile. Cheerful is a grim word to describe him.

He wasn't especially bright, and his saxophone playing was one of the reasons I still can't stand the instrument, but his happiness was so broad & genuine that to be with him was to be happy too. When he smiled, which was almost always, it made you feel better. Eddie's smile could make you forget a toothache. He was good to be with, and I liked him a lot.

One weekend—it must have been early 1948—my parents & sisters took off to visit our Uncle Gus in Miami. I was excused from the trip because Gus & I always clashed. So as not to be alone in the house—a pleasure I had not yet learned to enjoy—I invited Eddie over to spend Friday night with me & go swimming Saturday in nearby Ortega Creek. Spending the night was, probably still is, a standard part of high school life, and I had no ulterior motive—for the last time.

The family left while we were still at school, so when we got home, Eddie & I had the whole house to ourselves, a fairly heady experience. We spent the afternoon struggling through flute & sax duets. Then I cooked hamburgers while he made a salad, and we ate. The evening was spent helping Ed with his algebra. This involved sitting very close together at the dining-room table, with lots of physical contact, which I enjoyed but otherwise thought nothing of.

At bedtime, for a cheap thrill, we decided to sleep in the master bedroom. Although there were four beds in the house, two of them in one room, we never considered sleeping in separate beds. Sharing a bed was a standard component of spending the night. (When I think about this now, it amazes me that the whole world didn't grow up queer.)

(I realize now that there must have been some sexual element in our decision to sleep in my parents' bed. Can't see how there couldn't have been. I wasn't conscious of it, though, and I'd be willing to swear that neither was he. But there were many things about Eddie I never learned.)

The master bedroom was at the front of the house, facing south. Under the open windows was a hedge of night-blooming jasmine, and the air was thick with their heavy, horny fragrance

The moon, furthermore, was full, shining silver through the windows like jasmine scent made visible. A set-up.

We stripped to our shorts & went to bed. The night was hot, so we didn't use blankets or sheets: nothing covering us but a light sheen of sweat & the moonlight.

We lay on our sides, face to face, he on my left, awake but unspeaking, for what seemed a long time. His sweet boy-smell mingled with the jasmine, his pale body shone in the dim light. Then at length he touched my lips & with his delicate long fingers traced the outlines of my face. I mirrored him, his every move.

And there we lay another long time, speechless, nothing moving but our fingertips gliding gently, softly, over each other's bodies, head to waist (no lower), waist to head, slowly, slowly, in the jasmine moon. Without noticing when it started, I became aware that I was trembling, and so was he.

Without warning, Eddie slid his hand all the way down past my waist to my crotch and lay it firmly, not quite grasping, on the eager hardon I'd developed unawares. He rolled on top of me, straddling my left leg, and, keeping his right hand firmly in place, ever so gently humped my leg.

Now things became odd. When he stopped humping, I tried to roll over on him & reciprocate, but he resisted this. I tried to get us both out of our shorts, and he resisted this. I tried to put my hand on his crotch, and he resisted that, too, but I was determined, and stronger than he, and reached my goal. Then I understood.

Eddie had the genitals of a little boy. A defect of hormones, of course, which probably explained his over-all boy-ishness and certainly explained his reluctance to be groped, his embarrassment at nudity. It also probably explained why he took the lead in our erotic games.

Next morning I was burning with desire to see the naked Riley, and confident that circumstances would arrange that for me. We got out of bed (not mentioning what had happened between us), ate, rolled our bathing suits in towels, and set out for Ortega Forest.

Ortega Forest—I rode past it on the train this spring; it's been turned into an expensive subdivision—was a standard semitropical jungle, one of the loves of my young & hitherto urban life. Spanish moss-draped tall pines & oaks, palmetto thickets, strange vines & flowers, big yellow & black spiders with webs too tough almost to break, variously colored small & shockingly large lizards, orchids, fungi, rattlesnakes—a wilderness it was, my very first wilderness, and a most exciting place to be. Gone now, of course, as all things go.

To get to the beach, you had to trudge & slither through a mile of this prickly tangle, which made the beach exclusively young male territory. Consequently bathing suits were optional, if not downright superfluous. For an Irish-Catholic boy with a nudity hangup it was an island of terrible freedom in a sea of no.

It was not at the beach that I expected to see the Riley bare. If he wouldn't take his shorts off to fuck, I knew he wasn't about to go naked in public. But somewhere before we reached the beach we were going to have to change into our bathing suits, which couldn't be done without at least a momentary flash of nakedness. This was the circumstance I'd arranged & was counting on. We could, after all, have worn our bathing suits under our pants.

But Eddie foxed me. While I was looking at an orchid, he hid himself behind some trees & changed. Coming back he did the same, and I gave it up.

Never did I see him nude. Never did I finger his wee cock

or rub my palm across the silken bare skin of his ass. Though he spent the night with me once or twice a month thereafter till I went away to college, never did we talk about what we did in bed. A very strange relationship altogether, but somehow typical of my sex life ever since.

The Korean War broke out during my first semester at college, and Eddie Riley promptly joined the Army, once more compensating for his lack of genital development. I've often wondered how he coped with the compulsory nakedness that's so basic to the military life, and with the jokes & comments that must've been heaped on him by his fellow soldiers.

Still making up in heart what he lacked in balls, Ed was a good soldier. (I got all this from his mother later. He & I never wrote.) He made sergeant in record time and was assigned as an instructor to a base in Japan. In 1951, while he was teaching a bunch of recruits how to handle grenades, somebody pulled a pin. Eddie threw himself upon the grenade, saving the lives of a dozen men. His mother showed me the medal.

Overcompensation.

I mourn him still.

Now that the erotic ice was broken, I became a sex maniac. I never again slept innocently with anyone, and I slept with everyone I could. I didn't always score, but I always tried, and I scored more often than not. Golden days.

Next came Eddie Bronson. He wasn't in the band, but he was in my homeroom and my Latin class, and he lived only four or five blocks from me.

My red hair tropism began with Eddie. His hair was so incandescently red that his skin—unusually pale for a North Florida boy—looked almost greenish in contrast, and his eyes *were* green. A classical redhead, and in all ways beautiful. He was a little taller than I, slender, lithe, good to look at, good to touch.

Eddie was, necessarily, a crypto-sensualist. His family were rigid fundamentalists, stupid (as I thought then) but agressively "nice". I never saw even the smallest display of affection at his house, but every time I visited him lemonade & magnificent cookies appeared.

Eddie was fully as bright as I, and his family understood him fully as well as mine did me. They never, however, gave him the kind of high pressure static I always got at home, and were unfailingly kind. They wanted him to be a preacher (mine wanted me to be a priest), while he wanted to be an astronomer, but they never tried to force him.

Life being strange, he ended up as a mortician.

Ed & I rode, generally, the same bus to & from school, shared the same homeroom &, that year (1948), Latin class, and saw a lot of each other. Finally in October an upcoming Latin test provided my opportunity, and I invited him over to study with me & spend the night.

He came over, we studied, played a few games of chess, and in due time went to bed. I was very excited. I knew—I was determined—that something was going to happen, but I had only the vaguest idea what.

We lay there side by side, untouching, chaste in our boxer shorts, for what seemed a long time. Even in the moonless dark his body glowed. Perhaps, keyed up as I was, I was seeing Eddie's aura.

The house grew still. Eddie's breathing took on the regularity of sleep. I imitated sleep as best I could.

When I judged it was time, I rolled over casually, as one will in sleep, and let my left hand come gently to rest against

Eddie's hip. He jerked sharply, then lay still. I lay still as well, uncertain.

When nothing happened and it seemed clear that he was still asleep, that that sudden jerk had been involuntary & unconscious, I, likewise still asleep, allowed my hand to slide easily upward & come to rest upon his firmsoft flat belly. Oh, the drunkenness of flesh on flesh. I let my hand stay there a longish while, savoring. Eddie did not move.

Then idly, unconsciously, no fault of my own, my left hand eased down to the waistband of his shorts, paused briefly at this obstacle, savoring, then moved on to discover the first fully grown erection of my career.

I was delighted. Someone else's cock always feels so different than one's own. This one, rock hard & yet soft, was pressed tightly against his belly & pulsing. Otherwise Eddie still lay motionless.

I explored his hardon at my leisure, first traversing it repeatedly from outside his shorts, tracing the junction of head & shaft, the enlarged & ready urethra, details I'd never noticed on my own. Then I plunged under his waistband & through his fluffy jungle to the very base of his prick, discovering the transition point between soft flesh & firm, my hand all this long while moving slowly as a tide.

Abandoning caution & pretense, I skinned his shorts off and experienced for the first time that charming cooperative hump of the ass. I flew out of my shorts as well and there we were, in one of my ideal situations, two naked boys on a bed.

I lay on my back again and moved over so that we were in contact from ankles to shoulders. Again that struck bell trembling. I took his near hand & set it on my cock and once more seized control of his. We stroked each other for a while, mirror images again, slowly, as our excitement grew until our cocks were leaping under each other's hands like rabbits. Changing then from soft stroking to firm grasping, we masturbated each other until we came, explosively, scattering hot drops of semen all over each other.

Then, panting, we lay still again, come-smeared hands still holding on, while the Clorox-smell of semen filled the air, until our cocks reluctantly grew limp.

"Whew!" said one of us.

Naked & dripping, I sneaked to the bathroom for a towel, with which we wiped each other dry. Then we put our shorts back on—accidentally trading in the dark—and fell asleep holding hands.

Next day we both made A on the Latin test.

Eddie Bronson & I became addicted to each other. We slept together every chance we got, practically every week, even essaying daring daytime meets in risky places. At first we were limited to mutual masturbation, but as my adventures with other boys expanded my experience & imagination— to my knowledge Eddie never slept with anyone but me—we became gradually more sophisticated.

And no one ever guessed what we were up to.

Next came Raymond Harrison (no more Eddies in this tale). Raymond played sousaphone in the band. Another redhead—that makes three, you'll note, and thus my tropism was firmly established—he was shorter than I, stocky & muscular, brown-eyed, and tanned all over. He was a year younger than I, so we had nothing in common but band, which was enough, and the fact that he was bucking for West Point with every expectation of success.

He lived almost 20 miles from school, out near the Navy Base, so when the band gave a concert one unusually cold night in January, it was only natural that he come home with me. Otherwise, going all the way out to Hunters Inlet, he wouldn't've gotten to bed before 0200, and he'd've had to get up at 0600 to go to school.

When we got home after the concert it was, for us, quite late, at least midnight. The house was in darkness, and we hopped into bed quite without ceremony.

We lay there, as had become my wont, till each c'd be sure the other was asleep, and then I made my move. My left hand reached his hip, and then his stomach, and he brushed it away! My first rebuff. It seemed that he was still asleep—he was lightly snoring—and so I tried again, and was rebuffed, and tried again, obnoxiously persistent.

Eventually he stopped pushing me away (which probably meant that he was awake). I paused to consolidate my gains, then moved down to his crotch. No erection (maybe he wasn't awake). I squeezed the head of his cock gently between thumb & index finger, released it, squeezed again, and the cock responded, stirring, straightening, stiffening. Soon it was as hard as anyone c'd ask, which was the first time I'd ever done that to anyone but myself.

"What do we have here?" he said, startling me.

"Umm," I answered.

Raymond was certainly awake now. He quickly pulled off his shorts, then reached over & pulled off mine. Another first, and I was becoming somewhat disturbed. Things were moving too fast for me, I wasn't sure what direction they were moving in, and my accustomed role of gentle aggressor had been turned upon me. I'd encountered my first non-virgin.

Naked we lay there & played with each other. Then, fully in charge, he rolled me over on my side, facing away from him. He hugged me close, running his hands up & down my body.

"Oh, baby, baby," he moaned.

He spat on one hand, smeared his cock with the spittle, and slid his cock into my unexpecting asshole as easily as slipping a hand into a pocket. There was no pain—boys' assholes are amazingly elastic—just a warm sensation that grew ever more intense & pleasurable as he fucked. Another first, and one I didn't at all understand at the time.

All the while he moaned & whispered in my ear, held me firmly in his strong arms, moved his hands across me, jerked me off, fucked me first slowly & deeply, then faster & deeper, pushing us both upward through level after level of ever greater ecstasy, till we both came in convulsions of peak sensation, bucking & bouncing, making God knows how much noise that no one heard.

I'd been fucked, and very well fucked, too.

After a while he said, "You got a towel?"

I made my usual foray to the bathroom. We wiped ourselves clean—I've no idea what my mother made on laundry day of all the oddly stained towels I threw into the hamper—and fell asleep, exhausted.

That was my first more or less mature sexual experience, and—can you believe it?—several more years were to pass before, in the Dallas YMCA, I finally understood what Ray had done to me. Next day I suffered from a runny white diarrhea, and yet I didn't connect it with what Ray & I had done. The idea of the anus as an organ of pleasure was alien to me.

Even the words I use to describe the act were foreign to me then. The lace-curtain Irish curse was strong on me. Though I must have heard it before then, I was 19 years old the first time I said 'fuck'. My speech was anything but vulgar, and my thinking reflected my speech. I never swore, and neither did my friends. Boys who did were low class and, however lovely, much to be avoided. It's a wonder that I ended up as healthy as I did.

A few months later, Raymond & I slept together again, and this time it was different, and altogether typical of myself at that time.

The Philadelphia Orchestra, on tour, came to Jacksonville, and Raymond & I went to the concert, with the usual arrangement for him to spend the night at my house after. All the way home on the crowded bus, at his urging, I sat & he stood beside me, and all the way he kept rubbing his crotch seductively against my shoulder. We both had massive erections, and I was sorely embarrassed.

In bed, when the lights were out, he said, "I hope you're not gonna play with my peter like you did last time. You get me hard as a brickbat. How're *you* doing?" and put his hand upon my cock.

I was thoroughly offended. This was something to be done, but not to be talked about, especially so coarsely. And I was still annoyed from that embarrassing bus ride. So I got out of bed, turned on the desk lamp, and worked for an hour on a term paper that wasn't due for weeks yet. Then I went to bed & slept the unimpeded slumber of the pious & the just.

I was a fool.

The third time was at Raymond's house in Hunters Inlet. I was there to go swimming next day in a pond on the property. It being late spring & torrid, we slept nude, another first for me. Raymond didn't start anything, so I did, the usual penis fingering. Eventually he said, "Don't you ever do anything 'cept play?" I thought that meant he wanted me to stop, so I did. We never slept together again after that.

Raymond, Raymond! Had I known, my every orifice would've been your playtoy.

Raymond graduated high school, went to West Point, was commissioned, went to Korea, and died defending a hill that no one really wanted.

By late '48 I was experiencing failures as well as successes, failures of two sorts.

The first sort were boys who declined to play. Howard Littrell & Don Garvey, trombone players from our band, and Charlie Fox, a gorgeous bassoonist from Jackson High, were typical. On some pretext I'd get them to spend the night with me. In bed I'd make my move & they'd resist, finally rolling over on their stomachs to protect their tender parts from my predations.

These were not only failures but mistakes, for they talked. Without my knowledge, I was getting a strange underground reputation at Lee High. This led to the second class of failures, boys I neglected to take advantage of. These I regret to this day.

First of these was Allan Scott. Scotty was maybe the brightest kid in school. While still a junior, he was taking correspondence courses from the University of Florida and summer courses at the local junior college. He was also well known to be "fast". Girls warned each other against him. Mothers looked on him askance.

Scotty was a friend of mine, and of most of my friends. We bright kids stuck together. One night, at a party, he put an arm around my shoulders and announced, "Johnny, you can spend the night with me anytime."

A few weeks later, I did. He turned the event into an Occasion, a high class two-man party, going to great lengths to entertain, impress, charm and, had I but known, seduce me. In his rather lavish room we played chess & records, talked at length & brilliantly, examined his treasures, and between us downed a quart of scuppernong wine. The wine, my first alcohol, was a mistake. Instead of making me amorous, it knocked me out, and nothing happened.

Next came, or didn't, Richard Billingsley, our solo clarinettist. I was totally in awe of Dick. He'd gone out for football, then dropped out of the varsity to play in the band. He had the exaggeratedly perfect body of a footballer, a square & handsome face, laughing eyes (brown), auburn hair, and the largest cock, relaxed, of all the few I'd seen. He was also, later gossip informed me, amazingly horny, but too timid to do anything about it.

So was I. We spent the night at his house once, slept together daringly nude, and nothing came of it. We were each too shy to make the first move.

Dave Carpenter was another. Of merely ordinary but quite satisfying beauty, he was the son of the town's most prestigious & wealthy Methodist minister, and played third cornet very poorly in the band.

One day he & I & some others went swimming at an isolated beach on the river. The talk was all clean-worded but raunchy, and the playing all roughhouse & grabass. Openly covert, if I can be allowed such a construction. At one point while I was lying in the shallows, Dave slid over me & settled down, cock to asshole, head to head.

"Rrrr," he growled into my ear.

"Alligators in the sun," I replied.

The others laughed. Just a little more innocent roughhousing.

That night I slept at the Carpenter manse, and the only thing that kept us apart was the determinedly upper crust sleeping arrangements. We slept in adjoining bedrooms, an open door between us. If we'd slept together, we'd've done a good deal more.

Under such luxurious conditions, I had no idea how to get us together. Neither did Dave. He kept making strange noises that I wasn't going to understand for another two or three years. If he had once said, "Why don't you sleep with me?" or come in saying, "Can I sleep with you?" it would've been different. But he didn't, and neither did I.

Be it noted that none of the above survived Korea.

Sometime between Harrison-1 & Harrison-2, circumstances —I think it was a night rehearsal for an upcoming band festival—arranged that I spend the night at Susan Thomas' house. Suzie was my second flutist, and she lived in a large old house a block from school.

I normally spent a lot of time at Suzie's house anyway. Her family was enormous, poor & extravagantly happy. Five of the kids were grown & gone, but the other five, and their friends, kept the house lively. All were or had been in the band, and the band's social life centered on the Thomas house.

Mrs. Thomas was fat, dumpy, homely, cheerful & endlessly loving, an absolute mom. The house & everyone in it basked in her warmth. She was even a great cook. (My life changed as much when I discovered good cooking as it did when I discovered sex.) The contrast between her & my own dear mother . . .

I spent a lot of time there.

Mr. Thomas was a mechanic & inventor. He had a machine shop in the nearby slum and was only home at night & Sunday. He was always tired & less than clean, understanding & fair. It was his place, and when he was there everything centered on him, naturally, without his dominating anything.

In the late '50s he was going to be well off, but in the '40s there was never any money.

The Thomases were poor.

None of us noticed that the Thomases were poor, they always seemed to have so much more than any of the rest of us. There was never any trouble feeding an extra mouth, or ten. Between meals, snacks & sandwiches were always available for any number. No one was ever unwelcome. Almost never were there only Thomases sleeping or eating there.

Mr. Thomas built the house himself—there was nothing practical he couldn't do—and designed it to house a family of twelve. Three stories tall, it had ten bedrooms—many of them at this time converted to other uses—upstairs, and on the ground floor an enormous livingroom with fireplace, bookshelves, lots of battered furniture that didn't mind more beating, and a piano; a very large kitchen & pantry; a large diningroom with an heirloom table that could feed the whole family plus guests at once, and the parental bedroom & sewing room. Bathrooms scattered about conveniently. I've never been in a more comfortable house.

All the Thomases were musicians, and so were all their friends. Every gathering there was a concert. We could—and did—assemble 20-piece chamber orchestras there and play Mozart symphonies. And all of us were bright enough to do other things as well. We produced, for home consumption, two plays & a G&S operetta, plus plays & music of our own.

As I said, I spent a lot of time there.

Of the kids at home, the one I knew least was Martin, Suzie's 19-year-old brother. He worked at the machine shop with Mr. Thomas and was seldom home. When he was home, he played the best ragtime piano in the world.

Martin wasn't someone I'd've known at all if he hadn't

been Suzie's brother. He was coarse, for one thing, given to talking dirty & making sly allusions, and so were his buddies. He was widely known to be even more 'fast' than Scotty, and had once been suspended from school for having been caught fucking a cheerleader in the library storeroom. Furthermore, he had even Been In Trouble With The Law. Not my kind of lad at all.

But he *was* Suzie's brother, so I saw a lot more of him than I did of the other local toughs, and I couldn't help knowing that he wasn't all that bad. In fact, I liked him. We were, if not quite friends, certainly friendly. Besides, he was very good looking in a dark German way, with thick, sensual lips & slow, knowing eyes, and very mysterious in his more mature knowledge, and he played knockout ragtime piano.

So the circumstances that arranged for me to sleep at Suzie's that night arranged for the house to be crowded and for me to share a bed with Martin Thomas.

I went to bed before Martin came home, and fell asleep. Some time later he woke me by turning on the light, seeing me & saying, "Oops, par'm me," and turning off the light again. He undressed in the dark, and the sounds of his undressing—buttons opening, cloth sliding over flesh & landing softly on the floor, heavy shoes hitting the floor with a politely muffled thud, the ripping noise of a zipper, the long & frictive fall of pants—excited me.

He got into bed, the springs adjusting to the added weight. He smelled pleasantly of new sweat, grease & gin. (I didn't identify the gin till some years later.)

As we lay there side by side, inches apart, I could feel the warmth of his body impinging on mine. Time passed. I agonized over what I should do, what I dared to do. Martin obviously slept, his breathing heavy & stertorous. I did not realize the man was drunk.

Finally I gave up and sent out an exploratory hand. It found Martin's finely moulded thigh & swarmed across it to his large & flaccid cock, which quickly sprang to life.

So did Martin. "Honey?" he murmured. He threw off his shorts and rolled over on top of me, embracing me tightly with one arm while drawing off my shorts with the other hand.

He aligned our cocks and then, one arm around my back, the other hand cradling my head, thrust his tongue into my astonished mouth and began moving his hips, sliding his cock back & forth over mine.

This was all new to me, especially the kiss. I'd never tasted anyone else's saliva (tobacco & gin, the flavors were) and wasn't sure I liked it. But it was all part of one thing that I liked a lot, so I fell back on my old mirror image trick and did unto Martin as he unto me. My hands had free play over his muscular back, from the firm & plunging buttocks to the sweat-damp hair, and took full advantage of it. I could feel his heart beating strong against my chest. I was ignorant & nervous about it, but I was in heaven.

It was a hot night, and our sweaty bodies moved across each other with only the most pleasant friction. I was matching him thrust for thrust and things were moving quickly toward a climax when we heard footsteps on the stairs, Mrs. Thomas from the weight & pace of them. Martin froze. Nuzzling my neck, he whispered, "Don't be scared, honey. 'At's only ol' Miz Smith goin' to bed."

(Old Mrs. Smith was the legendary, and probably mythical, proprietress of the local 'cathouse', The Green Lantern, ostensibly a roadhouse & most likely nothing more.)

While we lay paralysed in each other's arms—Martin's weight on me, his pounding heart, a heady joy—the steps went past our door, on up to the attic, where they paused. Still we did not move. Then the steps came down again, past our door, to the ground floor, where they faded away to the back of the house: Mrs. Thomas making her rounds before going to bed.

Then Martin opened act two. He got up on his hands & knees—our bodies parting with a shlupping sound—spread my legs, raised my buttocks, and thrust repeatedly with his cock in the general area of my asshole, quite in vain.

If Martin had dealt with his own lubrication & aiming, like Raymond Harrison, or if I had understood what he was about, the night would've been even more memorable than it was. He was proposing to honor me with a really proper fucking, which would've markedly affected my subsequent career. As it was, I was more than a little frightened, and didn't know what to do.

Soon he gave that up and, dropping my ass back on the bed, crawled up on me until his legs were straddling my head and his cock was poking at my face. He rubbed it all over my face, but especially across my lips, persistently. Now I was not only confused but terrified.

Finally he gave that up too and rolled over & lay on his back. My fear, subsiding, was replaced by disappointment. Something very important had clearly not happened, and I didn't know what it was.

Tentatively, I reclaimed his cock & masturbated him. This, at least, I understood. Martin lay there passively, all except his cock, which responded eagerly to my handiwork. Suddenly, almost violently, he rolled on top of me again, and, sticking his cock between my legs, which he held together with his knees, he fucked me furiously for a few minutes, then came in great explosive bursts.

Then we slept.

I puzzled over this for several days, but could make nothing of it. There was no one I could ask, and I wouldn't've been able to talk about it anyhow. In those pre-porn days, there wasn't even anything I could read. It was very disturbing.

Next time I slept with Eddie Bronson, I reenacted the puzzling parts, playing Martin to Eddie's me, hoping he'd know what to do about it. Poor Eddie. Though he was willing to go along with anything I did, he knew even less about sex, especially this kind of sex, than I did. His reactions were the same as mine had been, confusion & some fear. Nor did I get anything out of the experience to suggest what Martin had done all that for.

Abandoning that tack, I returned to the interfemoral beginning of my Martin adventure. As we at first lay clasped tightly together, Eddie was still uncertain, even resisting at first the intrusion of my tongue in his mouth. But as I moved upon him his uncertainty faded and he responded with ever increasing vigor, until we must have been making so much noise it's a wonder my parents didn't break in to investigate. (That would've been a traumatic & memorable incident, to be sure.)

Well matched, we came together in a last burst of creaking springs & slurping noises, smearing both our bellies with a gooey coating of semen, and then fucked on a little longer just because it felt so good.

"Oh, that was *nice*," he said. He'd never before said anything in bed.

And it *was* nice, very satisfactory. It became our preferred mode of intercourse, and remains mine to this day.

So. I had learned a new sexual technique, and a good one, too, but I still had no idea what was supposed to have happened that night in Martin's room.

The next time I slept at Suzie's house—in a room of my own this time; sharing a bed had been unusual—I waited until the house was quiet, then sneaked into Martin's room. This was uncommonly bold of me, but I knew Martin wouldn't raise a fuss. At the worst, he'd ask me to leave him alone, and in light of our last adventure, even that seemed unlikely.

Martin was easily stirred to passion. The moment my furtive fingers touched his cock, it arose in all its majesty. I was even more impressed by its size than before. Neither I nor any of my other lovers—I didn't think of them as such at the time—had anything to match its girth or length.

Once again Martin flew out of his shorts. I was crouched beside the bed, and he dragged me onto it almost brutally, stripped me, and threw himself upon me. He fucked vigorously for nowheres near long enough, then rolled off, grabbed my head, and shoved it into his crotch.

"Kiss it! Kiss it!" he hissed, pushing my face down on the glistening huge prick. "Kiss it!"

"How did you get such a big one?" I asked inanely.

"Kiss it!"

So, reluctantly, I kissed it, the same sort of tight-lipped dry peck I'd give my mother or any relative, which was all the word 'kiss' meant to me so far.

"Kiss it!" he repeated, trying to shove the swollen head in past my closed lips & clenched teeth. Then, "Shit!" he let me go & fell back on the bed.

He didn't fuck me anymore, but passively allowed me to jerk him off. When he'd come, I sneaked back to my own room, and that was that.

The next time I tried anything with Martin, he said, brusquely, "I don't feel like no boy ass tonight," and that was the last time.

I feel sorry for Martin now. He must've been horribly frustrated. All he wanted was to get inside something soft & warm & wet, and all I knew to offer him was a hand job he could've done as well himself. But if he'd just explained what he wanted me to do, told me how, it would've made us both a good deal happier.

By my senior year I was getting laid, after my fashion, at least once a week. This was quite an accomplishment for a 17-year-old boy in those days. What's more, though I slept out every chance I got, most of this intense sex life was carried on at home, in the very presence of my determinedly anti-sexual family, without their suspecting a thing.

Indeed, it wasn't till four years later, in Memphis, that they first entertained the possibility there might be something odd about me. A lover of mine fell in love with my sister. Whilst balling me, he courted her. But she'd have none of him, so, vindictively, he told all in a longish rambling letter that I wish I could've saved.

Concerned, my parents took me to a shrink, a solid Catholic psychiatrist recommended by our parish priest. He gave me a battery of tests, had me on the couch for half a dozen sessions, and then solemnly assured them there was nothing wrong with me at all. That settled it.

But back to my senior year. By then a lot of my sexual ignorance had eroded away. I realized by then that what I was doing was sex, and I'd stopped going to church, mainly to avoid the embarrassments of the confessional. But I didn't think there was anything especially unusual about what I was doing. After all, all of my closest friends did it too.

But I'd become very curious about sex per se. No information on the subject was to be had at home, and such sexual lore as I got from my peers even I knew better than to believe. Though I had some friends, like Martin Thomas, who could've told me everything I wanted to know, I was too embarrassed to ask. What I needed was a book. I've never anyhow trusted any information I couldn't find in print with cross references. But sex education books were hard to find in 1949.

I had a weekend job shelving books at the main branch of the public library (where, by the way, I first met quite a few of my lovers). This job gave me the run of the place, including the locked shelves. There one afternoon I found a new book, one, it must have been, of the first modern sex manuals. I promptly slipped it into my briefcase, sneaked it home, and surreptitiously read it twice, the second time just to be sure, before sneaking it back onto the shelf.

And that's how I found out I was homosexual.

With all I'd heard about queers—my father used to tell stories about beating up queers, ugly effeminates in women's clothing—I should've been terminally distressed by this discovery, but I wasn't. In fact, I was quite excited, even pleased. Anything my parents spoke so ill of had to be good.

Next time I was alone with Eddie Bronson—poor Eddie, I really put him through a lot—I pushed him onto a sofa and, fully clothed, started making out with him. When we were both properly heated, I broke the news.

"Do you know what we are?" groping him enthusiastically. "We're homosexuals!"

"No!" squirming, "No we're not! Don't talk like that."

"We are," my hand inside his pants, and his in mine. "I read it in a book."

He insisted that we couldn't be, and kept babbling that he'd spend the night with me any time I wanted. Even after I made him read the relevant parts of the book he wouldn't believe it.

(I spoke to Eddie twelve years later on the phone. By then he believed it.)

So I knew I was homosexual, and it made no difference to me. I also knew that I wasn't queer, wasn't a fag. Two years later, in Dallas, when I first associated with other homosexuals, I learned that I wasn't gay either.

And I'm still not.

Well laid & content with my lot, I graduated high school with an A- average, maybe thanks to the convenience of having friends over to study. That fall I went off to college. That winter my family was transferred to Memphis.

I never saw any of my high school lovers again. When I came back to Jacksonville next, almost five years later, all of them I could trace but Eddie Bronson were dead, killed in war or accidents or crime, and he was out of town. It's as though my whole generation was wiped out, and I only am escaped alone to tell thee.

But they remain my lovers to this day. Their echoes, like ghosts, throng this book, my bed, the parks & streets of everywhere, unchanged, unaged, immortal in my arms.

I suspect I'm much like you.

FIVE

1969–1977

6/25/69 — L.A.

Fingers were made before fucks.

My fingers conduct my sex life for their own purposes &
pleasures. Perhaps it's *their* sex life and they let me share it.
Even when excessive speed shrinks my cock to flaccid thumb-
size and makes orgasm unthinkable, I am able to enjoy rich &
rewarding sexual experiences based wholly on touch & feel.

(This is probably what I've heard called 'infantile eroti-
cism.' So be it. I submit, first, that it's far superior to no erot-
icism at all, which is what the alternatives generally boil
down to in practice, and second, that long after my genitals
have aged down to exclusively excretory functions, my fingers
will still be able to ravish every body they can reach.)

My fingers were neatly programmed for sexplay long
before sex itself began to interest me. "Touching" and "Feeling" were the cardinal sins my mother drummed upon inces-
santly from the first day they were possible on up through the
last time ('63) I saw her in 30 years of unflagging obsession.

Oh. And "Looking." In fact, especially Looking. The
worst (nondestructive) sin she could imagine was to look
upon somebody impurely. ("Impurity" was the word. Most
of what it meant was "Naked." Naked bodies were per se
impure.)

Yet I never did come to be much of an eye fucker (except
in the sense that my aesthetics are visual). Of course, I've
always "Looked," in my mother's sense, every chance I got,
but, even looking at bodies in my bed or candidates, even

with the most uncompromisingly sexual motives, looking has always been aesthetic for me, not erotic.

Your eyes can't do anything but see. Sight is separation. Abstract. Passive. Nothing doing.

So I've never done much with my eyes. (Maybe wearing glasses all these 30 years has kept me from it.) Dirty pictures do not turn me on. Beaver mags don't move me. Nude photos are not people. Naked people (unless accessible) are nice enough, but seeing them isn't at all the same as fucking them. I'd rather have one good body at hand than 100 in view.

(But I seem to have a latent gift for voyeurism. A little patch of skin exposed unawares—the small of someone's back whose shirt, he crouching or bending over, has crept up— excites me. Any body that doesn't know I'm watching I can watch for hours. The secret of voyeurism is secrecy. So I suppose I *could* become an eye fucker after all. I only need practice.)

Looking's pretty but touching is real.

Anyhow, I was carefully programmed from the playpen on to Looking & Touching & Feeling erotically, and I entered sex young through those doors. (Mother never told me fucking was sinful—she suggested as much but never had the nerve to come right out & say it.)

Looking was first, at 5 or 6 in Quincy, Mass. A friend & I, summer days, would go to a nearby granite quarry, to the scrap pile—50-foot fissured heaps of irregular boulders, among which was a room, a cave, large as a kitchen—where we'd play at striptease for hours. One would go outside, the other wait within. Outside boy would remove one or more garments, inside boy would try to guess what. He generally stripped, but I was chicken.

(Another thing about Looking: it's better the more it's

forbidden. And a guilty secret is a pleasure shared.)

This kind of eyeplay continued, according to opportunity, as my sole erotic practice till '46, in Dallas. At Greiner Jr. High School, phys. ed. (never before in my life) locker room mass nakedness sort of discharged the energy of looking. Naked bodies ceased to be what my mother had made them. They were no longer special.

Sight works at a distance, but touch is right in there, intimate, therefore harder to arrange.

I mean, you & a buddy can go to the pool, say, and while you're changing into or out of bathing suits it's perfectly proper to see & even look at one another, and as long as neither of you gets an erection the erotic nature of this looking can be ignored, and is. But if you stick out your hand & stroke his silken ass or tenderly squeeze the head of his astonished prick, the quality of the experience becomes precise, and you'd better be able to explain if asked.

It's the difference between watching & doing, passive & active. Nothing doing versus doing something.

"You can look, but you mustn't touch" is supposed to be the rule.

(Samson Shaw was the most beautiful object at Robert E. Lee High School during my senior year, a trumpet player. When I took him swimming at the Officers Club, in the dressingroom he went to outrageous lengths to keep from being seen, paroxysms of naked modesty. Alas. Yet, some year later, standing outside the bandroom one night after a concert, five of us including Samson, he allowed me under cover of darkness & in accidental mode to grope him thoroughly (cock waxing to ivory & trembling) for more than half an hour while we talked about I never knew what. Strange reversal, and I never touched Samson Shaw again.)

Danny, 18, a Cancer, who lives in the Barker House.

We did this before, in December, 1971: the full treatment, both drunk on mead, naked on my narrow bed in the back room of the Ukiah Street house. Several hours of incessant sucking & rubbing & belly fucking & body surfing, with hundreds of microcomes but not one come. Thorough, detailed, delightful, and I've lusted for him ever since.

This time started this evening, sevenish, downstairs in Miranda's shop. I'm drinking a beer. Enter Danny & his brother-in-law Steve. Beer in my left hand, right hand hanging at my side.

Danny sidles up to me, covets some beer, reaches for mine, grinds his crotch against my right hand. Surprise. When this happens, you know that something's up.

I give him my beer—the least I can do. He takes five minutes' worth of sporadic sips, maintaining firm hand-crotch contact all the while.

Shy (we have an audience) I finally retreat behind the counter. We & Steve talk trivia. After a while Steve says he has to split. Danny goes with him, saying he'll be back later if it's all right with me. I allow as how it is.

Danny walks Steve as far as the corner, one-third of a block, then turns about & comes back. Right on.

Upstairs. I ask him if he'd like to get terribly drunk. He says yes, and that he already contains 1½ sixpacks.

I mix pseudo-Collinses: 1 oz. medicinal alcohol, sugar, water & lemon juice. We talk some about this. It's a bizarre drink, and the flavor takes getting used to.

We move to the front room, love seat centered on the big picture window, fat moon gleaming on the Bay & throwing silvery light on silvery Danny (he's a pale Okie). There is talk about music. He asks if I have any pot. While I'm rolling two joints, there's a disturbance at the door—someone I mean to fuck tomorrow.

Back to the front room & more music talk. He wants to be a musician. I foolishly offer to teach him enough to get him into a music school. We smoke the joints & drink some pseudo-Collins. His leg is constantly pressed against mine, and still we talk music.

To the piano, two on the bench, close quarters. He plays "Heart & Soul" & I show him some of the things you can do with C-Am-F-G, none of which he understands, and how to hold his hand to play a chord. He's not sure what a chord is. I hope he doesn't take my teaching offer seriously.

Back to the love seat & stoned, drunken silence—moon on the water, moonchild on my right. My right hand plays with Danny's nape, a long time. I'm torrid.

I say, "Remember the last time we were drunk?"

"Yeah."

"Bet I c'd make you come this time."

My right hand rests on his shoulder. He reaches up, takes it, and transfers it to his crotch. Of course.

I exploit the situation, rubbing & groping & stroking at length. Eventually I get his pants open & repeat the process with only his shorts between me & his cock.

Then contact, skin on skin. I get pants & shorts just far enough down to let me in. First I rub, then I suck for at least an hour in as many different ways as there are. During this I get his pants &c below his knees (he's being semicoy) and manually annex everything from knees to nipples.

He almost comes a hundred times—enough so I can taste it—but never quite comes once.

"Your hand," he says.

All this time we're on the love seat. Though I've managed to turn the light out (who needs it with such a moon?) I haven't been able to get him into bed, or even onto the floor. Claims it might bring him down. So there he is, sitting upright in the moonglow like a statue of King Tut, with me on my knees between his legs applying every penile stimulus known to man. I hadn't realized the extent of Danny's narcissism. He's entitled.

Enter fat Barbara in the midst of a suck, causing no disturbance. She sees what's happening & exits quietly.

"Your hand," he says.

So I jerk him off for another long time, in every way two spit-slick questing hands can find, taking all other available liberties as I go.

He almost comes a hundred times—my hand is lightly sprinkled—but never quite comes once.

(At the very beginning, the clothed grope phase, I said, "You know, we don't have to be drunk to do this," which may have been true.)

At last he says, "You see?" and things slow down. We give it up. He pulls up his pants and, groggy, splits.

God is good. What a fine show for the Solstice.

Maybe he will tell his friends. Danny has some very pretty friends.

Drink is the curse of the sucking class. What I did to Danny would have made a statue come.

8/12/73

Last night, full of complex lusts, I went around the corner to the Uncommon Good, seeking whom I might devour. The UG is always good for this. Downstairs it's a folk/rock coffee, beer & wine house, multiply useless for my purposes, but upstairs it's a pool & pinball parlor where the local kids hang out, and the local me as well. The kids drink surreptitious beer, shoot sloppy pool & try, awkwardly, to make out. I just drink beer & make out. Seldom do I leave alone.

Whom I might devour tonight is Danny once again.

Danny is so lovely it almost hurts to look at him. Fair hair glinting gold under the pool table light, pale eyes, face white despite a long & sunny summer, long, lean, clean lines emphasized by clothes so tight I don't know how he can move in them. Tonight he's wearing a bright yellow T-shirt (his tiny nipples bulging through the taut fabric, muscles & motion on intimate display) and skin-tight faded Levis faded even more around the crotch, obviously no underwear. The cock I know so well shows forth in faded blue, the elegantly indented buttocks flex with every move.

He's stretched out blue & gold across the green table, shining contrasts, erotically stroking the cue. He shoots (how beautiful), misses, yells "Shit!", turns away from the table, and sees me watching him. He smiles.

There are other puppies in the room, most of them lovely, but from the moment Danny smiles there is no question whom I'm taking home tonight. It's a lax & horny smile that, along with the easy shot he missed, informs me Danny's drunk again. Shit, I think, another sisyphian night. But no matter. Danny doesn't have to come, as long as it's me he's not coming with.

Danny turns back to the game, overtly ignoring me. Covertly, though, he's more than aware of me, and it's really the game he's ignoring. Even when it means missing a shot, he strikes all manner of poses designed to turn me on, which they do. Between shots, not looking at me, he strokes his crotch, licks his lips, brushes back his nearly invisible hair, smiles. If he's not careful I'm gonna throw him down on the pool table & rape him in public, which'll probably get me 86-ed from the UG.

The point is, which I realize & appreciate at once, that Danny is seducing *me*. I am charmed.

Thanks to his drunken ineptitude, the game doesn't last long, though it seems to. When it's over, he comes up to me and says, "Hey man, you got anything to smoke at your house?"

"Got some hash," I say, "and a bit of opium."

"Oh yeah?" He lowers his voice & says, "Let's go."

We go.

Downstairs I pick up a sixpack & we break out into the shining night. It's eleven o'clock. Danny puts an arm around my shoulder & we stagger down the hill to my house, he rubbing catlike against me at all times. We're only moments away from public scandal. I couldn't be happier.

Barbara moved out a month ago, so we've got the house to ourselves. This has never happened before, and I take care to point it out to him. "Good," he says.

First I go to the john, then he goes while I play the piano, bracing myself. Nothing's happened yet, and already it's unbelievable. He takes what seems to be a long time, and then comes into the front room gloriously naked, already half erect.

"Sure is hot tonight," he says, which isn't literally true. "Why don't you get comfortable like me?"

Indeed, why not. I shed my boots & socks & stand up to remove the rest of my clothes. Danny comes up behind me & reaches around me, helping me undress. Four buttons & a shrug & I'm shirtless. His hands snake to my crotch, rub & linger, fumble with the belt & zipper. One hand enters my jeans & grasps, tingling, my cock, the other slides my pants down. Two kicks & I'm bare & ready.

His hot breath whispers in my ear, "I never done like this, you know, with anybody else." I have nothing to say.

We stand there in the starlight, front to back, his slightly roughened hands sliding from my neck to my balls & back as mine are wont to slide. His cock is fully up & pressing against my butt, not trying to get in, just staying there, a few degrees warmer than the rest of him. We sway back & forth, getting a palpable electric charge from each other.

A hand moves to my face & gently strokes it in profile, in outline, tracing eyebrows, lips, jaw. The ghost of Eddie Riley stirs in me. Then he turns me around—this is Danny's show— and we stand face to face in a classic full clinch. Kissing deeply—where did he learn this shit?—we masturbate each other slowly. He's breathing hard, and so, I guess, am I.

This goes on for a long time, during which only strength of will keeps me from coming all over him. His cock-throbs suggest the same is true of him. Perhaps he's not as drunk as he let on.

Finally we separate—the sweat we've generated makes a sucking noise as we do—and he says, harshly, "What about that O, man?"

Dope break. I set up a candle on the picture windowsill while Danny, gold & silver, glides around the room. Jupiter, low in the sky & brilliant, shines full on us, striking occasional lights across his sweaty hide. I load the pipe, sit in the well-named love seat, and say, "C'mere."

He sits crosswise on the seat, his upper body on my lap. I put my left hand where it'll do the most good, and with my right hand heat the pipe over the candle flame. When it's smoking, I slip the pipestem into his mouth, saying, "Here. Smoke this."

He sucks in a bushel of smoke, goes rigid in my arms, then relaxes with a long sigh. I do the same. It's really good opium.

After a while he says, "Oh wow," and then, "C'mon." He leads me by the hand into my bedroom, and I see why he'd seemed to take so long in the john. He'd undressed in my room & turned the blankets & sheet down on the bed.

We collapse in a heap on the bed, making a thump that must've wakened Miranda downstairs, and then for hours we crawl all over each other, every inch of each's skin coming in contact with every inch of the other's.

At one point we're locked in an impassioned 69. It's clear he's never done this before—too much tooth—but he's eager & steadily improves. Thanks to the opium, this goes on forever, and we both come again & again to the brink of orgasm, and again & again back off from it.

Then later, somehow, I'm fucking him in the ass. Thanks to a Navajo called Eli, I do this very well. Danny is moaning & squirming, saying "Oh Oh" and "That's good" and "More more," and breathing hard. I'm holding on with my left arm & hand across his chest—those tiny, hard nipples, that silken skin, velvet muscles—licking & nibbling his nape & ears, and with my right hand masturbating him with all my skill, trying to transmit my cock's pleasure to his cock.

And this too lasts forever, until I say, "Danny, I'm coming!"

"So am I. Don't stop!"

I wasn't about to. Then we come, within a half second of each other, copiously, noisily, and this too lasts forever. And then, still joined, we both pass out.

I woke up first and lay there a while, staring in amazement at this beautiful boy on my bed. Silken Danny. The room smelled of spunk, come, boysweat, opium, a heady blend. He seemed to shine with his own light.

My hand learned Danny had a hardon, and I went down on it slowly, gently, lingeringly. "How fine to pass from love to sleep, and how much finer wakening to love."

He seemed at first to be asleep, but then his legs rose over my back, clamping my head between his silver thighs. I went on sucking, musing on how velvet-soft a hardon really is. His heels rubbed against my back, his hands rubbed my shoulders, upper arms & head, first languidly, then faster & harder. Then his thighs tightened convulsively, his hands pushed my head down on his cock, and, screaming, he came in buckets of oddly sweet-tasting semen.

Later, while we were washing up, his joyous body still open to my eyes, I said, "I told you I could make you come."

He only smiled.

Seduction implies that the subject eventually submits voluntarily. The purpose is to bring the subject to say yes. Not to go against the subject's will, but to induce the subject to change his will. Seduction implies a certain amount of sportsmanship & fair play.

Ideally, the seduction sh'd lead to the subject's wanting to ball, not just agreeing to.

You can seduce a boy by playing on his sensuality. Back rubbing is an honored approach. My energy transactions sh'd also serve.

Or by working on his curiosity. Get him to wondering hard enough what it w'd be like, and you can generally end up showing him what it's like.

(The 'boy' I'm talking of is no one boy, and not all boys.)

A really horny boy is quite easily seduced.

You can seduce a boy by awing him with your wisdom (this is the Guru ploy) or by making yourself the object of his hero worship.

(What is meant throughout by 'a boy' is 'some boys.')

You can seduce a boy by discussing sex with him. I used to do very well with discussion/demonstrations. We'd ostensibly be talking about balling chicks & how to improve one's performance, and I'd describe & demonstrate things that feel good, showing him both how to do them & how they feel. Nothing compromising to begin with, but progressing at a rate established by the boy. Progress was usually total.

(Often in a well-directed discussion of homosexuality, a boy will allow as how he'd kind of like to try it w'ldn't know how to go about getting it done. But not often enough.)

Sometimes it suffices to make it easy for the boy to seduce you.

You cannot seduce a boy who doesn't admire you.

You can seduce a boy by salesmanship. Convince him it's at least worth trying.

You can't seduce a frightened boy, nor an abnormally insecure boy, nor a defensive boy. You can't seduce a very short boy.

It's easier if the boy is tired, but not if he's exhausted.

Heads & California city boys present special, but typical, problems, which are, in the former, impaired response/affect, and with the latter, excessive sophistication.

You can't seduce a hustler. (However, it's not especially hard to get a hustler to donate his services.)

It won't hurt if the boy knows you are strangely attracted to him.

The more excited you can get the boy before you strike, the better the chances.

Diffidence is no aid to seduction. If you can't bring yourself to ask for what you want, you're unlikely to get it.

Pornography doesn't seem to be good for anything but to introduce the subject.

(A boy who introduces the subject himself is no problem.)

The boy must be put at ease before you can begin. He sh'd feel comfortable, and be glad to be with you. Even somewhat flattered by your letting him join you.

The boy sh'd feel good, the better the better, and the feeling sh'd be clearly identified with you.

Generally, an assortment of conditioned fears will have to

be shorted & grounded before anything can be started. You're trying to enlist his cooperation in an act he was surely brought up to consider unnatural, unthinkable, & hazardous to the health. This can be turned to advantage if the boy has already begun to question his early conditioning.

Fear of sex itself used to top the list, but that seems to be dying now. Next, fear of homosexuality. This is fear that he might be changed by the act—'queered' was the word in my day. Depending on the degree of his inexperience, he may be afraid the act will be physically painful.

He may be conditioned to think such acts disgusting &/or degrading. He may in ignorance be horribly afraid of what unknown nameless things you want to do to him, or expect him to do.

All such feelings have to be forestalled before they arise—after is generally too late. You must have the boy's trust. You must be wholly admirable in his eyes. It must be obvious that nothing you might do w'd be disgusting &c, that you w'd never hurt him. It's always good to establish early that (when it comes to it) you don't generally go in for this kind of thing, but such is the strange & powerful attraction this exceptional boy exerts on you that you just can't help yourself. (This must be subtly done, but it's not difficult.) Every boy w'd rather be the irresistible exception in your love life than your standard fare. He'd rather his were the only cock ever you'd sucked. (In this connexion, it furthers one to be 'bisexual.' Many boys who'd never bed down with a faggot have no such prejudice against bi's.)

In any case, the whole event sh'd be somehow made to seem as special for you as it is for him. Nothing routine, matter of fact, commonplace or ordinary. A touch of exaltation sh'd run through the whole affair. Everything heightened, ecstacy-prone.

(A few simple procedures of Magick c'd be of service in many instances. Room decked out as a true sorcerer's chamber. You full of ecstatic, clear, compelling explanations of whatever he asks about—stressing, unless otherwise indicated, that nothing supernatural is involved, no superstition. Tend to encant when you speak. After a proper build, demonstrate. Give him experience of Magick via energy transactions, formal incantations & maybe an invocation, projection, easy mind/imagination exercises, whatever fits/works, to induce in him unprecedented mental states, feelings & experiences tending to predispose him favorably toward your desires. Given a fairly suggestible boy, this procedure c'd prove spectacularly effective. Introduce the lad to simple sex magick.

(It's often helpful to demonstrate an Oracle for him—let him throw a Change, or read his cards. Be as circumspect in your interpretation as integrity allows, and be advised that the Oracle will generally tell you what may be expected from the boy. My *I Ching* record is full of Changes thus generated.)

The boy sh'd know that he's special, that it's not every boy you'd let into your room, or talk thus to, und so weiter.

Be not overeager, nor overly familiar or handloose, but warm & avuncular. Be the classical nephew-molesting uncle of everyboy's youth.

If you can blow his mind, you can probably blow him as well.

It w'd further me to reactivate the old charisma, to dwell in ecstacy once more, radiate joy, to shine in full daylight. Resume the Haight persona.

Do what you can.

Poor boys are easier than middle-class or rich ones. Boys who've been busted are easier than boys who have not. Southern boys are easier than Northern boys.

Marines are easier than masturbation.

It's no use trying to lead the boy around to making the suggestion himself (though it happens, sometimes). His self-esteem won't allow it. In support of his unblemished manhood, it has to be the other guy's idea.

Even considered in the most favorable light, to invite another man to bed & ball is a slightly gay thing to do, though to accept such an invitation is perfectly all right. (Rationale: I really do need a piece of ass, & this is all there is.) The situation demands the most delicate juggling of Yin & Yang.

But when the lights go out, the rules go too.

(A boy who accosts you on the street & asks you where the women are in this town does not have to be seduced.)

If, on the other hand, the boy structures the situation as a dominance/submission relationship, the need to protect his self-image is considerably less. The scenario calls for you to sweep him masterfully into the sack and there use him gloriously. (This takes more nerve than I possess, and if there's any doubt at all, I play it safe.)

You sh'd at the outset sound the boy deeply, by questions, observation & intuition, and determine if you can his safely pushable & panic buttons and make judicious use thereof. You sh'd also reacquaint yourself with the universal button pattern, so as to be able to improvise.

A boy who will go with a strange man to the stranger's room is already half seduced.

What a boy w'd rather die than do with a faggot he'll generally do fairly readily with someone who, sex prejudices aside, does not seem to be gay. (Then again, there are some boys who prefer flagrant queens, but I don't know anything about those boys.)

Boys who have toward older men the sort of thing I have toward boys are supposed to be quite common, but I've only known two. What fun it w'd be to know more. (I suppose any boy who strongly prefers the company of older men is a candidate.)

A little alcohol, not even enough to feel it, is all the excuse a lot of boys need.

Theoretically, both parties to a seduction sh'd participate actively in the balling. But if the boy still has reservations, it does not further one to force them.

7/11/73 — Mendocino

Massage is a sovereign technique of seduction. Not irresistible, but tending powerfully to forestall resistance. It introduces the element of sensuality before any thought of sex arises, making its appeal not to will or desire but to present experience. It avoids the intellect, speaks directly body to body. It is an intimacy of which sex is merely a further degree. A sexual act in itself, the consent to which is easily, naturally broadened & extended. It obviates discussion & the weighing of values.

The difference between massage & a sexual caress is a matter of never more than twelve inches in one direction or another, a matter of carrying a stroke one easy step beyond propriety. And if it leads to sex, that sex is greatly heightened & enhanced thereby. And if it doesn't, massage is its own reward, and a worthy one. License to feel a lovely body at great length & intensity & in great detail is not to be gainsaid.

(I don't rub enough backs anymore. Even where seduction is unnecessary, prolonged massage sh'd be my rule. Rubbing bodies is fun, and I'm good at it. Why have I let this practice lapse?)

Dope's another powerful seduction tool, but far, far from infallible. The original superstition of our early doping days, that pot leads directly to bed, died young. As a sensual stimulant, though, in conjunction with either repressed desire or a good massage, it goes far to incline y'r subject toward y'r wishes. But it doesn't bludgeon inhibition down like alcohol. It's more like a seasoning.

I'm a puritan. That says I will (& so far have) never have sex with any boy too young to get a hard on. It isn't necessary for the lad to display an erection throughout the event—the steadfastness of the younger cocks is proverbially vagrant, and the body is so clever that in the transitory absence of a rod there's still no lack of things to do—only that he be able to display an erection at all.

I haven't had much access to brand new cocks since (a) Travellers Motel (b) Wogglebug—either way 8 to 10 years ago (discounting the affair of Schultz in Charleston, or Carl the 16-year-old STPer in NYC last fall: both young enough but jaded). This is too bad, really, for I'm fairly fond of young boys, the younger (see above) the best (though Ronnie at the Travellers still has me thinking that one wants something more from a 12-year-old—what I cannot say—than cynical enthusiasm). (For instance, that still air of supernatural conspiracy with which, at that age, we used to conduct these affairs.) (Or—let's be dirty—the trembling of fear & lust & excitement & inner conflict & trust with which my maraudings in high school (and analogous situations since) were often rewarded: a boy whose surrender is half an inch ahead of my fingertips.) Twelve is still too nearly childhood for me. Sexually blank. Responses & delights—in Ronnie, anyhow, and, logically, in many more—were generally inappropriate & hollow (outlined rather than faked), freezingly immature reactions—not surprising, considering that he'd just lately been 11 and his genitals were still a child's.

Point is, I'm not really a child molester at all. I don't much like children, not even socially. Alien: they do not think, value, speak or feel the way I do. Feh! Children.

Teen-age boys! gentlemen. There's the drug that's ruined me. It's that lust made me what I am. That's the appetite that spoiled my chances for a successful, happy life in the real world of the majority. My sick dark tropism, my preoccupation with high school cock: that's the game that's had me burn my years in city slums passing joints to runaway fingers while around me the company's grown every year duller, more numerous, less musical, more criminal—Puppies! my friends; it's puppies are my curse, gentlemen. Puppies & methedrine.

Both harder to get hold of every day.

For a Friday the 13th it wasn't half bad. My 15 mg Dexedrine spansules had arrived from Berkeley in the morning mail, and I'd taken three of them at five or six hour intervals and was moderately wired. I devoted this ersatz energy to pounding the typewriter until just about 11 p.m.

I'd just got home from Mendocino, where two or three glorious puppies had tried to thrust themselves on me, whom sadly I'd had to reject for lack of a private place to dally, and I was unconscionably horny. I'd've been willing to have sex with Boris, the big red dog across the street, faut de mieux, but I was hoping for better things. I had, after all, six bucks in my pocket, and c'd afford to drink at the Animal Farm in Crystal Creek & see what might develop. If that didn't work, Boris w'd always be there when I got home.

So at 11 o'clock I abandoned my typewriter, donned my brown suede jacket (abandoned in the San Jose hospital emergency room by someone unknown who presumably died there & didn't need the jacket anymore) and plunged into the darkness out of doors.

As I walked the mile to Crystal Creek, I repeatedly informed all appropriate entities the purpose of my walk was to get laid.

The Farm was fairly crowded: no stools empty at the bar, two tables & a bench occupied, but lots of room to move around. There was luckily no band.

I went directly to the cigarette machine at the far end of the room for a pack of Tareytons. This gave me an opportunity to reconnoiter without appearing to be cruising.

It was a pretty standard shaggy Friday crowd. Bearded men & pallid women in flashy rags, people in urgent need of a bath, tottering drunks pretending to shoot pool, a young German shepherd & a Doberman pup disruptively romping around one of the tables—a few people I knew & a lot I didn't want to, with some overlap. Crystal Creek high life.

There were four points of interest. Three were together, blond boys, one short, one medium, one tall, looking much alike, probably related. They were sitting on the bench near the front of the room, whence one or the other of the shorter two made pretty frequent forays to the cigarette machine or the juke box. The tall one never moved. Brothers, I suspect.

They were pretty enough, and I entertained fleeting notions of a four-part adventure. They all had thin faces & long hair. The short one, who was obviously in charge, had a small goatee, darker than his hair, and was dressed in orthodox western hippy garb. The middle one was similarly dressed, but had no beard. The tall one, who never moved, was clean-shaven and wore a red&white striped shirt, like a football referee's, and whitish yogi pants. He was barefooted; the others wore boots. They all moved in the slightly effeminate manner of psychedelic vegetarians, and their faces all wore the blank, entranced expression I associate with Scientologists & Jesus freaks. They were neither of these, however, for they were all smoking cigarettes & drinking what were probably mixed drinks.

As I said, I entertained a brief fantasy of luring them all to Willow Grove & molesting them singly, in tandem & en masse. Then I thought on the logistical difficulty & general unlikelihood of such a project, and turned my attention to the fourth possibility.

Another blond, he was sitting, apparently alone, on the last stool at the front end of the bar. Though, sitting down, it was hard to tell, he seemed to be about my height. He was wearing a new-looking straw hat, Levi jacket/shirt, Levi's & boots, and c'd easily have been a ranch hand. I unobtrusively eased my way toward the front of the bar, checking the kid out.

At the bar I got a Bud, then went out mid-floor where I c'd keep an eye on the ranch hand—and the three brothers, just in case—whilst seeming to watch two drunks play at pool. Now & then a surge of people w'd flow around me, and at the end of each surge I was closer to my target than before.

He still appeared to be alone, but he had at least one friend there, a short, mustachioed Mexican. The friend wore Levi's, a horizontally brown&yellow striped T-shirt, and a brown leather gaucho hat. He was either drunk or demented, maybe both. He capered about, ape-like, maybe dancing, and played games, juggled, with his hat. He made me think of organ grinders.

At quarter of twelve, long before I came within talking range of my ranch hand, the Granada County Sheriff's Department paid its regular visit, two burly deputies trying to look hip. They were between me & the ranch hand. There was nothing to be done until they left, twelve-fifteen.

Now I was within striking range, and he & I were aware of each other. He had his feet up on an otherwise empty stool on his left, and seeing me hovering, he put them down & invited me to sit.

Granada County fox & hare.

I ordered another Bud. He thrust out a hand & told me,

"Bill." Not wanting to go through the usual rigamarole about Johnston, I took his hand & replied, "Jack."

"Chuck?"

So much for avoiding the rigamarole. We rang phonetic changes on 'Jack' until I finally spelled it for him. He explained he had trouble hearing, due to a Vietnam war wound.

We talked. He didn't want to talk about the war, so we talked about the drought, about rattlesnakes, dope, the usual small talk of strangers chance-met at a bar.

He told me about his buddy, Andy. Andy was fucked up in his head, thanks to the war, and given to freaking out. Bill was ready at the first sign to go to his aid. He & Bill had been partners a long time, before & during their Army time and ever since. Bill thought a lot of Andy.

"He was the best partner I ever had, but he got fucked up. He ain't much good anymore, but he's still my partner."

He wouldn't say how Andy'd been fucked up, nor did I really care. I was more concerned with how to separate them, how to get Bill into my clutches & Andy out of the way.

We talked. Bill was Bill Clark, 24, a Capricorn, married with one child. Andy was also married, and Bill had brought him to the Farm over Mrs. Andy's strong objections. Bill was reared in Kentucky & West Virginia, but now he & his lived on 25 acres he's paying for between Loma Mar & Pescadero. He's an apprentice blacksmith & also drives a '73 Peterbilt, a more or less gift from his father, on which he has only $16,000 more to pay.

Bill's as pretty as needs be. Another thin-faced blond, the musculature of his face is somewhat skew, cheeks bulging oddly out above his narrow jaw, echo maybe of some childhood Appalachian dietary problem. More than adequately attractive, thanks.

We talked a while, ordinary bar talk, hard to separate from all the other bar talk I have known, for maybe ten minutes. Then he said, "Can I ask you a question? Real flat out?"

"Have a good time," I told him.

"Are you gay?"

Flat out indeed. Normally I answer this question with lies, but this time I said, "Yup. Does it matter?"

It didn't matter. He just wanted to know. Things were looking up.

Now the cards, some of them, were on the table, and it was up to me to play them as well as I could. This was much more interesting to do than it would be to write or to read about. Mainly I worked by indirection, being charming & friendly, showing flattering interest in everything he said, being brilliant, witty, wise & interesting. Valentine shamelessly snowing a pup.

Bill played some cards of his own. In the most casual manner possible, he would talk about some close, dear friend from his past, who happened to be gay. At this stage of the game, one c'd get the impression that all of Bill's best friends were faggots. The implications were not lost on me.

Meanwhile the noisy, capryllic life of the Farm swirled around us. Andy seemed to be getting it on with Linda, a beautiful but drunk & neurotic girl I sometimes play recorder to.

Bill told me that tomorrow he had to drive his truck from here to Reno & back, leaving around 0730. I said it hardly seemed worthwhile to go to bed, the time being so short. I also implied that I might be able to help him stay alert on the drive, delicately hinting at Dexedrine.

(I was aware of a number of small inconsistencies in Bill's

story. The reputed wives, for example, didn't seem to harmonize with Bill & Andy's presence at the Farm, nor with Bill's increasingly obvious coming on to me. I didn't let this worry me.)

About this coming on: Bill had taken to elaborate tongue games & knowing leers. He also managed to accidentally touch my upper legs & knees repeatedly, and to maneuver me into touching him (no problem there). Neither of us hinted that his being an attractive male & my being gay suggested possibilities beyond the Farm.

It became a quarter of two.

"This place is about to close," I observed. "Do you really want to stop drinking at two o'clock?"

I told him about the beer, whiskey & marijuana at my house, and he showed interest. He noted that Andy seemed to be in good hands (Linda's). I asked if Andy c'd fend for himself without Bill, and he avoided the question, but his tongue play increased considerably. If I hadn't been rapt up in all his games implied, I might have thought them grotesque and wondered about his mind.

He seemed to suggest that if we split now we c'd get back before Andy missed us, which I didn't & still don't understand. What I did understand was that somehow we were going to do exactly what I wanted to, Andy notwithstanding.

At a time when I wanted to keep my attention firmly fixed on Bill, Linda sat beside me & started telling me, incoherently & too softly, about something horrible she'd seen earlier in the day. Andy followed after & talked with Bill. I strained to hear their words while seeming to listen to Linda. No good.

The last call came. Andy got a six-pack. Bill said it was time for them to go home now. Complications I had not allowed for. Unwilling to give up with my prize so maybe near, I asked for a ride to Willow Grove. Granted.

We drove to Willow Grove in Bill's pickup, and I invited them in for a drink & some dope. Accepted.

Andy settled himself with a can of beer in my swiveling arm chair. I made myself a drink, Fleischmann's Preferred on ice, and got a glass of water, all he wanted, for Bill. We sat at the table & talked.

I gave Bill three spansules, one to take then, the others at intervals after. He complained of a back ache. I asked if a backrub would help and he said that he'd love it. Andy fell asleep. Good old alcohol.

(Bill also complained of colon problems, meaning basically constipation—we'd discussed this before at the Farm—and I looked up a lower bowel tonic in Dr. Christopher's book, which I'm now engaged to compound for him against his return Sunday or Monday.)

We retired to my room for some therapeutic massage. He insisted on darkness, and that we cover Andy with a blanket or something. My bathrobe sufficed.

I asked Bill to take off his boots, jacket & shirt, and lie down. He did this, and undid his belt & unzipped his Levi's as well. We still didn't mention sex, but all subterfuge was gone.

So, unbooted & shirtless, I rubbed Bill's back. It was a splendid back to rub, with all the contours & textures I so love. When I rubbed low on his back, he humped to give me access to his ass & shove his pants down.

A lovely ass, an elegant ass, an ass of many noble qualities & delights. Somewhere in *Sheeper* someone says it: for asses it's boys, women for tits—which I think half right. I do get off on boy ass, and on puppy nipples too, whereas tits have nothing to offer me.

Still rubbing (rubbing backs is sexual per se), I began to take tantalizing liberties, Bill making sounds of pleasure all the while. I rubbed slowly down his flanks from armpits to hips, sensually, all pretense of therapy dismissed, fingers in-curved to miss no contours, no details. And again as I got below the waist Bill humped to grant me access to his belly & the outer fringes of his thatch. Throughout I moved as slowly as I could, savoring, teasing, sensitizing, turning Bill ever further on. His pleasure noises were as good to hear as his fine young flesh to feel. I'm an awful lecher, but I try to give satisfaction.

When I asked him to turn over he wanted more back action first, which he got. Finally he rolled over unasked, and there were all his beauties spread before me.

I gave his front as much attention as I'd given his back, moving like a lingering tide up & down the continent of his flesh. I circled his nipples with in-spiraling strokes. His neck, face, shoulders, the insides of his elbows. I brushed his cock with casual, soft, feather strokes, up & down, brushing the sides, not yet grasping it nor even fully touching it, leading it on.

It was a good cock, one of the best. Fairly long & proportionately thick, but not impossible, circumcised, rooted in a surprisingly small patch of hair, elegant & responsive. A cock to which I'll happily return, if I may. And it was as glad to see me as I it. It bounced & jumped up to meet my touch. This was a cock that firmly expected to be sucked and was looking forward to it. In many senses, a grateful cock.

For me it was like coming home after a long absence. Not since February had I so much as seen a cock, a naked boy, a willing body on my bed, and here lay one of the very best examples of all of the above. Such a wealth, this Bill Clark: rain after long drought, boyflesh after loneliness.

The entities I'd evoked en route to Crystal Creek had come through in high style & glory.

I lightly rubbed Bill's wand with one hand whilst removing his Levi's—that last fiction—with the other, Bill cooperating. He was having a good time, and so was I. Then I lowered my mouth over the head of his cock & double-tongued it like a flutist in frenzy, entering upon the first phase of a virtuoso blow job.

Which was exactly & all that I had in mind: a virtuoso blow job. I, after all, was fresh & unbathed from a waterless week in Mendocino, and maybe too wired for an erection of my own, more interested in being fucked than fucking. Further, Bill being married & ostensibly straight, a grand but simple blow job was all I expected him to want, which I was overjoyed to provide.

Bill had other ideas. While I mouthed ever gradually further down his happy shaft ("Oh, that feels *good*," he said, and would say repeatedly thereafter), Bill squirmed around until his hand c'd reach my crotch. Then he groped me, rubbed me, opened my pants.

I didn't allow my astonishment to interfere with what I was doing. Furthermore, I managed to get rid of not only my trousers but also my T-shirt without skipping a beat or missing a stroke. (I don't know how I do these things. When they happen, I'm always too busy to notice.)

After more squirming, Bill had us in classic 69 position & my limp prick in his mouth. I tried not to think of what my week's worth of stale crotch sweat must smell like, comforting myself that Bill was maybe too drunk to notice, which was probably not true.

The Dexedrine had indeed unmanned me, and what Bill had to suck & play with was a flabby length of hollow flesh

& not much more. But he overcame this chemical handicap like a pro, and we soon had equal mouthfuls of pulsing hardness. He blew me well—not as well as I was blowing him, but far better than I'd have expected from a man who was married & probably straight. He blew me so well, in fact, that, to my own surprise, I came. I hadn't been blown to orgasm in more years than I remember. My ranch hand knew his stuff.

This led, however, to a short discussion break. Bill was irked that I'd come in his mouth without warning him. I pointed out that I'd been much too busy sucking him off to warn him about anything, even if I'd thought he'd needed warning, and asked him what he'd expected me to do with him sucking away like that. "When you suck a cock," I said, "you've got to expect it to come. Otherwise what are you doing it for?"

This settled that, and I returned to my own project, Bill Clark's ivory cock.

Bill squirmed around again so his head was on the pillow and I, impaled upon his rod, lay between his legs. These he lifted and rested on my shoulders, cradling my head, my ears, between his silken thighs while I plunged up & down his holy cock. (This is one of my all-time favorite sexual postures.)

Shortly he rolled us over so we lay on our sides.

"Do you want it?" he said, almost belligerently. "Do you want it all? Can you take it all?"

Unless he was capable of unprecedented miracles of further expansion, I already had, so I looked up from my pleasure & said, "Do it. Give it to me." And we went on as before.

Bill was not a quiet lay. He kept murmuring, sighing, "Good. Oh, good. That feels so good." This didn't bother me at all.

Up & around & down & around & up I slid on his burning pole. My tongue performed prodigies. My hands wandered, explored, stroked his velvet buttocks, gently fingered the cleft, his small tight asshole, followed the line across and cupped his balls, he squirming gladly all the while.

"You give a better blow job than my wife," he said. I was glad to hear it. His wife's name is Lynette.

We rolled over on his back again and I used my hands to supplement my mouth. I got his cock all slimy wet and swept my palm across the head & down the shaft and swallowed him again, repeatedly. He liked it.

And so it went for two exacting hours. After a while, maybe the first 45 minutes, I understood he wasn't going to come. This certainly wasn't my fault and I didn't let it bother me. We were both having a glorious time, and if he'd come (much though I value coming) it would only have ended our fun. Nevertheless, I did my best to bring him to climax. It was the least I c'd do, and I was willing to do much more.

(Andy, meanwhile, was not a quiet sleeper. He talked loudly: "You bitch! You bitch!" He groaned. He thrashed about noisily. He drummed his booted feet upon the floor in a possibly dance rhythm. He made a lot more noise than we did, but didn't have a fraction of our fun. Well into our second hour he grew so loud I couldn't see how he failed to wake himself up. Several times we thought he'd done just that, and we stopped until his sleep breathing resumed. The last time this happened, we both fell asleep.

I awoke after a while (good old speed) to find myself snuggled closely with a warm & naked boy of exemplary beauty & exuberant sexuality, and I was happy.

(In these accounts I strive to make my writing as pornographic as I can, within the limits, loose ones, of a reasonable prose style. I delight in hoary dirty-book cliches. I revel in elaborating details of what is essentially a very simple act with few available variations. I gloat. And this for several reasons, the greatest of which, dear reader, is to arouse *you*, to give you (be you male) a rollicking hard-on, to fuck you with my words, and (be you straight) to make you for the time it takes your cock to rise and fall as queer as my queer self.

(Another reason, not much less: to make these lovings live for me. This is my album, these my trophies. The time will likely come when these my words on paper will be all the sex I have, when these paper fucks will be the only fucks I get. Then will I cherish each overwritten, sweaty page, and dwell on every purple detail, all so much alike, so individual. Then I'll have incredible erections, comings, golden flesh on flesh, the thrustings, odors, sounds & tastes, the varied hairs & groins, hard muscles & soft skins, the feel and wonders of a thousand boys, all rising in my mind when long my body has forgotten.

(And what will you do, when you're old?)

In this happiness I slept again, an hour, till speed & Andy's noise aroused me, rested, to my normal state of borderline paranoia. Bill slept soundly, as a well-sucked youth sh'd sleep.

My problem was this: granted that Bill & Andy were longtime partners, how much did Andy know about Bill's sex life? What if he woke up for real & stumbled into the bedroom & found his best friend cuddled naked with a naked me? No way c'd he fail to understand what we were about there in those arms, that bed. I knew not a thing about the man except that he'd been fucked up in 'Nam, not even what form his fuckedness took. How might he react, finding his buddy in my homosexual embrace? What effect w'd this have on their relationship? What w'd Andy do?

This was too much for me (though when we were actually fucking I didn't give a shit what Andy thought). I got up, got dressed, went into the middle room. Six o'clock. Andy sound asleep.

I proofread yesterday's typing till seven, when Bill woke up & joined me. We talked quietly, now quite openly talking about sex, what we'd done, his sexual career. Except for the fact that his first homosexual experience had happened when he was very young, whatever that means, none of this talk was especially informative.

We also talked, then & after Andy awoke, about Bill's problems. After being wounded in the head, for which he was drawing $126/month disability pension from the Army, Bill deserted & ran away to New Zealand. He was caught, shipped back, thrown in the stockade, court-martialled and given a Bad Conduct discharge "for the good of the service," all this back in 1972.

Now he was trying to get this discharge upgraded at least to GD/UHC. He asked me to help him prepare his brief, so to speak, which I agreed to do. So he's coming back Sunday or Monday with all his military records (and I hope without Andy). We'll go over them & then outline his case.

(I think he's got a good case, by the way. If his head wound was serious enough for the Army to give him a pension because of it, it was too serious for him to be properly ordered back to combat duty, which was what precipitated his desertion. Further, given such a head wound, there is some question whether he can be held responsible for his acts at that time.)

Now, this business of coming back &c might only be talk, but I certainly hope not. I have plans for Bill Clark. Unlike most of my lays, once with Bill is nothing like enough. At the very least, I want to do it again under more nearly ideal conditions. Me clean & tasty, no speed to dull my responses, no buddy in the middle room to keep our lid on (though he didn't particularly inhibit us this time).

I want to explore/exploit this erotic treasure at greater length & depth, in greater diversity. I have the idea there's little he won't do (oh—he wouldn't kiss me). I want to know this boy in every physical way he'll agree to, to the limits of our imaginations & capacities. I don't believe he'll bore me.

And I want to know him otherwise, as well. What sort of a person is this Bill Clark, happily married & a father, who lets himself be picked up in the Farm (insists upon it) by the first aging stranger who wants to, who clearly went to the Farm with roughly that in mind, who sucks cock skillfully and says he isn't gay, perhaps? (His own perhaps.) What is his history, what brought him about? I can only begin to list the things I want to know about this man.

And (supposing he does come back) we've already, almost fortuitously, established a perfect foundation for a prolonged & deepening relationship. Thanks this much to speed, I'm already cast as an older, wiser, more knowledgeable teacher-type man, more than willing to teach him just about anything he wants to learn, whose knowledge & experience of the world is attractively greater than his, and who furthermore gives better blow jobs than his wife Lynette. "If you want to keep a boy," it says in *Sheeper*, "you have to teach him something," and I really think I want to keep this boy.

I have fantasies already of taking him places, turning him

on to new experiences, new sensations, foods, ideas. Of him visiting me in Berkeley and going with me to concerts, museums, the Magic Cellar, restaurants. Of getting high with him on countless drugs of the very best quality.

And of endless, extravagant sex.

I wonder if he'll let me fuck his ass.

At 10:30 they left, presumably (at least Bill) to come back, and I began this record. May it be extended well & soon. I c'd easily develop a hangup.

AFTERWORD

Whatever impression the foregoing has created is necessarily somewhat misleading. My journal records only my fleeting, casual lays. The more enduring relationships kept me both too busy & too happy to take notes. This book records my lusts but not my loves. Those are recorded in heaven. As, doubtless, are your own.

John Valentine

Some other titles in our series of Memoirs by gay men are:

Jack Robinson
Teardrops On My Drum

Liverpool in the 1920s: still Dickensian in its poverty, a city of docklands and back alleys, barefoot kids running wild in the filthy streets, bizarre eccentrics and sectarian violence. This is the world marvellously evoked by Jack Robinson in the story of his boyhood: forced to fend for himself from the earliest age, searching the city for adventure, love and sex, and joining the army as a 14-year-old boy soldier.

'A fascinating autobiography with its evocative descriptions of life in the Liverpool of the 1920s' – *Time Out*

ISBN 0 85449 003 5   *£4.95*

Jack Robinson
Jack and Jamie Go To War

This second volume starts in 1937, with the 15-year-old hero back in his home town after his spell as a boy soldier. The action ranges from Liverpool under the Blitz, through D-Day, via New York, South Africa, and the Allied landings in Naples. It sees Jack as a wartime commando, then a seaman with the convoys, caught up in mutiny and racketeering, and always in pursuit of boys.

ISBN 0 85449 077 9

£4.95

Michael Davidson
Some Boys

Following on from his acclaimed autobiography, *The World, the Flesh and Myself*, this is a fond and revealing memoir of the author's many encounters with youths on his travels. Michael Davidson was a widely respected foreign correspondant, active communist and a self-confessed lover of boys. These recollections combine erotic intenseness with an unerring personal empathy, serving as a testament to the universality of homoerotic desire.

ISBN 0 85449 087 6 £5.95

GMP books can be ordered from any bookshop in the UK, and from specialised bookshops overseas. If you prefer to order by mail, please send full retail price plus £1.00 for postage and packing to GMP Publishers Ltd (M.O.), PO Box 247, London N15 6RW. (For Access/Eurocard/Mastercharge/American Express give number and signature.) Comprehensive mail-order catalogue also available.

In North America order from Alyson Publications Inc., 40 Plympton St, Boston MA 02118, U S A.

NAME AND ADDRESS IN BLOCK LETTERS PLEASE:

Name ....

Address ....

....

....

....